Fly
Diamonds

A.A. Dober

TO LORRAINE

My love and partner in life.

CONTENTS

ISBN: 0996549145
ISBN-13: 978-0-9965491-4-1
LCCN: 2016905609
A.A. Dober, San Diego CA

ACKNOWLEDGMENTS

Many thanks to my wife and children for their love. To the stories I heard of my grandfather which inspired this book. To Milton Avery for his beautiful images and his art. To pigeons and their amazing feats of flight. To the Editors at Kirkus that helped polish the manuscript. And to the border cities of San Diego and Tijuana that are easily crossed by pigeons but so tough on human beings.

PROLOGUE

On Forty-Seventh Street in New York City, between Fifth and Sixth Avenues, the diamond vendors dominate all other businesses. The one-block area is called the Diamond District, and Hasidic Jews travel back and forth among the shops, creating an ambiance similar to that of a Chagall painting without the beautiful colors and flowers.

The street is filled with buyers of diamonds as they run around shopping for a good deal. Some come to buy large diamonds that vary wildly in price, depending on quality. On average, a perfect stone of roughly 1.5 carats appraises for the equivalent of the annual income of a minimum-wage employee. Because a stone could seem good or bad to the naked eye, expert appraisers handle the job of distinguishing quality and value. Buyers routinely appraise a diamond they want by taking it to a so-called independent appraiser across the street. However, the idea that these appraisers are independent and that they can guarantee the quality of a diamond is illusory, because the appraisal businesses are controlled by the same families and friends who control the retail shops. It is an insider's game in which buyers rarely get what they pay for. So why do they shop in the Diamond District? Because they can get a good deal compared to the prices the jewelry shops on Fifth Avenue charge, and because it is hard to judge good diamonds with the naked eye.

***

On a wintry, overcast day, a lone female appears on the corner of Sixth Avenue and Forty-Seventh Street. She wears large, dark shoes with laces and a beige overcoat. Her hair is black and long, and a large hat covers most of her face. She walks like an old woman, and if people were paying attention, they would notice her strange quality. But it is a fleeting New York moment, and she is just another person on the crowded streets.

She walks into the Rapp Appraisal business and asks the attendant for an appraisal. He tells her to wait in the small anteroom on a cheap chair that looks like a leftover from a hotel ballroom. Finally, after twenty minutes, she is summoned to see Mr. Rapp. In his messy office full of papers and strange objects, there is a small area of leather, where Mr. Rapp assesses diamonds. She notices his black coat and white garment with long tassles that flow past his thighs when he gets up to greet her. He is a Hasidic Jew. She immediately pulls out a small black leather sack with a rock in it and sets it on the leather.

***

"Our standard fee is one seventy-five," said Mr. Rapp.

"My friend sent me here because you charged one twenty-five," she countered in a raspy forced voice. "His name is Martin Cetrero."

2

"You know Martin? Huh…OK, one twenty-five. Let me see the rock."

Mr. Schwarz took his loupe and studied the stone carefully.

"Nice one," he said.

The lady remained silent. Mr. Rapp weighed it at 705 milligrams.

"Three point five carats," he said.
"I am aware of that. Should bring fifty-five, right?"
"You a retailer? Maybe in retail you could get that."
"How much wholesale?"
"I can give you thirty-five, right now, no questions."
"Forty and it's yours."
"Hold on."

Mr. Rapp swung his chair around and opened a cabinet. Inside was a safe, which he opened simply by giving the door's lever a quarter turn. This transaction might have appeared to be unsafe, but the network of family businesses in the Diamond District provided extra security—escaping after a robbery was practically impossible. No robberies in daylight had ever succeeded, not in decades.

He took out four stacks of brand new hundred-dollar bills, wrapped in straps with the number "10,000" printed on their sides. In less than a minute, he had handed over forty thousand dollars for a flawless rock he could turn around and sell the next day at sixty-five, maybe even seventy if the color proved to be better than it appeared to be at first glance. The lady took out her reading glasses and checked the money carefully, quickly flipping through every bill. Her nails were short, her cuticles smeared with red nail polish. *Old age, perhaps*, thought Mr. Rapp. She placed the money inside the money belt she wore beneath her gabardine coat.

"Thanks," she said, then stood and left Mr. Rapp with a smile on his face that only a sure and quick profit could impart.

The lady took a yellow cab up Madison Avenue to Seventh-Eighth Street, where she got out and walked into a beautiful gallery with blue-chip Impressionist-era art displayed in its windows. Inside, she was greeted by the manager and escorted to a private office where the owner sat.

"I have the money," she said, handing him the four ten-thousand bundles.
"Good," the man replied, then began to count the cash.
"It's all there."
"I must, you know…"

She waited visibly uncomfortable in her attire standing up every once in a while to adjust her pantyhose in a non-ladylike fashion. When he was finished making sure the forty thousand was all accounted for, he handed her a framed oil painting of two white doves perched on a rooftop measuring nine inches by twelve inches. It was a 1955 piece by famed American artist Milton Avery.

"I wanted it unframed," she said.
"Yes, I know, but it's really a beautiful frame, and it protects it," he replied.
"OK," she said.

4

"You know he is the American Matisse."

"I am quite familiar with his work. Do you have my provenance papers?"

"Yes, of course," the man said, handing her an envelope.

She read the provenance and, satisfied, left the gallery with a wrapped package that fit in a shopping bag, crossed the street walking upright and firmly to a small Milanese shop called Sant Ambroeus, and had an espresso and a tiny sandwich that cost nearly twenty dollars. She mailed the provenance papers to her home and ended with two painted doves in a shopping bag that would fly easily in luggage to a far away land.

ONE

Juan Luis Merlo sat on an old sofa inside the living room of his mother's home in Tijuana. He visited on Sunday afternoon and onto Monday, his day off, making it a personal weekend of sorts. He limited crossing the border to once a week and spent most of his time in San Diego living in a rented room. Outside lay a pit bull on a chain that Virginia Rodriguez de Merlo kept for safety. Juan knew his mother liked the dog but that the two had a relationship that ended at the front door. Her home was just too clean to have a large dog living in it, and on top of that, it was small— Juan's feet barely fit between the coffee table and the sofa. Placing his feet on the coffee table was totally unacceptable to his mother. Even though the home wasn't hers, the living room was not designed to be comfortable, a concept one could only understand if one knew Juan's mom grew up in Mexico City where living rooms were seldom used.

In a few hours, he would need to remove the jacket, because the sun would raise the temperature to a balmy seventy-five. He was bored and grumpy, and he sat there, reading photocopies of pages he'd taken out of a cardboard box that sat next to the sofa. They were the

7

court papers from his father's lawsuit, which his mother would not let him remove from the home. Most of what he read only confirmed what he knew already.

On breaks, he stared at a wood imprint left on the ceiling during construction, just next to where the white-painted walls met the concrete ceiling. The walls were coarsely plastered, and they contrasted with the other finishes in a manner that most ordinary people living in the projects didn't care about. But Virginia was not ordinary. She kept bringing up the defects in the hope that one day Juan would learn how to plaster and fix them. Juan hoped to move her from the miserable home, which he was renting on a month-to-month, cash basis. He knew that if he didn't make the rent, the eviction process would be private, painful and he could show up on a weekend to find her on the street. The law in Mexico favored those who had possession, but with the type of landlord they had, a court-ordered removal was the least of his problems. Juan kept reading, but the depressing subject of the case, combined with his mother's living conditions, weighed on his soul. She didn't deserve this fate; her father had been successful, and she had come from an intellectual family.

She kept the living room spotless, even though there was dust everywhere just outside the walls of the little cinder-block home. Tijuana was located in a desert where water was scarce; grass and trees were unaffordable in the project. On the walls, she had hung the last indication of a better past—a collection of prints by Salvador Dalí. These prints were not only her pride and joy but also the first art she had purchased with her husband back when Juan was only two years old. Framed in elegant gold-leaf frames, they were a potential target for thieves. They were also a source of discomfort for Juan, even though art was rarely stolen in these parts since it was very hard to fence. Juan found it surreal that she cared so much for this little room that was almost never used. In the breakfast room, a hop away from where Juan sat, the TV was almost constantly on and permanently set on mute. It was a Sony Trinitron from the eighties but still worked perfectly and was like a mute companion for his lonely mother.

When Juan was only fifteen, his father, Diego Merlo, died from an alleged suicide that was propelled by a bankruptcy. The ten-year anniversary of his death was fast approaching, and Juan knew that it would be a blow to his mom. Grief had taken years of beauty and joy from his mother and had prevented Juan from achieving a proper education. Juan was smart, and this lack of opportunity also kept him wondering how far he could have gone had he attended a university. Only recently, his mother had shown him the paperwork of the lengthy court case that supposedly drove his father to his death. Juan missed his father immensely, because he had been a sensitive and kind man who had worked in the toy industry. Juan had grown up surrounded by new gadgets and gizmos that sometimes didn't even work, but interacting with his father as he tested the toys had been wonderful. On top of that, he never once felt unloved by his father. His father's absence and loss were like a punch in the gut for Juan, and discovering that Diego's death had been unfair intensified Juan's feelings. Juan sometimes lost his breath when confronted by these emotions.

Juan remembered that in the 1990s, before the great financial crisis and before 9/11, life in Tijuana had been improving rapidly. Manufacturing assembly factories called *maquiladoras* had been sprouting up everywhere, and entrepreneurs thrived by providing low-cost manufacturing to US enterprises. Few

Mexican businessmen imagined the hit that China factories would inflict on them. No matter how hard they tried to compete, the Chinese could produce better and faster, in larger quantities, and most important, more cheaply than the Mexicans. Juan's father had the clever idea that manufacturing on the US side meant that his toys could be labeled "Made proudly in the USA." He had plenty of laborers who would appreciate a minimum wage so close to Mexico. They earned dollars and lived for much less in pesos across the border. Diego's idea caused his business to thrive.

The Mexican population in San Ysidro and Chula Vista was practically indistinguishable from that of Tijuana, the only difference being the way of life. Juan's father opted to have the family live on the Tijuana side; he'd never liked living in the United States. Juan suspected the decision came down to friends and lifestyle. But within only five years, Diego Merlo went from a happy and successful man to a broken man. What had happened? The answers lay in the report Juan read.

Diego's factory had grown rapidly in size and output, so much so that it had been running twenty-four hours a day, seven days a week. He'd managed to achieve a level of growth that couldn't be overseen by himself personally; therefore, he was forced into leaving the factory in the hands of managers for two of the shifts, as well as hiring workers who sometimes were too inexperineced to know the difference between a hot press and an overheated disaster. Nevertheless, productivity had continued to grow, along with Diego's client list. He had even been starting to make small batches of toys for the big toy companies.

It was bad luck, therefore, that the factory caught fire in the early morning hours one Easter Sunday. Diego

was in the Valley of Guadalupe on a weekend outing,
wine-tasting with his wife. Flames ignited from a
combination of dirty rags and a hot machine oozing
leftover plastic that had been ignored by a careless
worker. On any other day but Easter Sunday, this
would have been a nonevent—the small fire could
have been stopped by a worker. But the factory was
empty, and thus it was a total loss.

Diego was accused of insurance fraud by his own
policy provider, the Tickell Insurance Products
Corporation, better known as TIPCO, which he had
thought was there to protect him. This huge and
powerful company became his enemy. Allegations of
misconduct and embezzlement, as well as accusations
that his business had been doing badly, appeared in all
the local papers. Juan remembered how devastated his
father had been, because he hadn't been prepared for
such calumnies. On top of that, he'd never had court-
system experience in the United States, and before he
knew it, all his money was exhausted on lawyers' fees.
Between no factory income and the legal expenses,
Diego was wiped out even before the trial date was set.
His lawyers were incompetent, and in little time, the
TIPCO power team had rendered them useless.

Then came September 11, 2001. On that date, life in
Tijuana changed forever. Just crossing the border into
the States became a three-hour ordeal. Diego Merlo
was broke, and, finally, he took a TIPCO settlement
for a pittance. He barely had enough to pay the lawyers
and ended up with nothing. The fire had devastated
him, and 9/11 had destroyed his vision of providing
US-made goods with cheap labor. Juan remembered
his father being so depressed he had wandered about
aimlessly, obsessing over how to recover from the
mess that was his life. One day, when he was walking
on the side of the great Tijuana River basin, a dry

concrete structure built to avoid flooding from the rare flash floods that occurred in the area, he slipped and fell, hitting his head on the concrete below. He was instantly killed.

Juan didn't believe that his father had intended to die—he had not been not suicidal. But everyone had known that he had been going through a rough patch. Therefore, his life insurance company would not pay out a benefit, because his death was ruled a suicide. Twice within a short time frame, Juan was gypped by TIPCO. His father should have been able to leave something for all the hard work he'd done. Years of inventions and manufacturing, all gone up in smoke, and the years of insurance premiums paid to insure his family could survive in the event of his death, all worthless.

Everyone claimed that Juan's mother had kept all this from him so that Juan could grow up happy and not be sad all those years, and perhaps that had been the right choice. But once he read the court documents, the truth hit Juan like a ton of bricks. He swore to himself that he would avenge his dad. But how? Being born on the American side and having two nationalities afforded him the possibility of a job that paid in dollars, though not for much more than that. He supported his mom in a simple and mediocre life on the Mexican side of the border, and that meant that he couldn't afford to lose his work in San Diego.

His mom worked by sewing every now and then, but her clients were few and typically paid late. On top of that, Virginia hated to work. She constantly told her son that without him, she would be finished. The reality of her needs created more than the normal emotional attachment a son had to his mother. Juan was not only a son but the surrogate head of household, like so many other underprivileged kids. Many times, she had expressed that they were not about to return to Mexico City with nothing to show for themselves. She preferred to lean on Juan instead of suffering the ignominy of facing her family and friends while destitute. Her prideful response was common in Mexico, though hard to sustain by those who fell on hard times.

Juan sat now, feeling the outside heat radiating through the window, choked up once again after reading the case files. He zoned out, and his eyes finally came to rest on the TV, which was tuned to a European variety show. On a stage, dancers and comedians performed one after the other to a large crowd of patrons sitting at dinner tables, much like a mix of the Golden Globes and *America's Got Talent*. A group of about seven television personalities sat at one of the tables, commenting and introducing the different performances. One particular gray-haired man was the main announcer. Juan grew bored with the show and popped a videocassette into the VCR.

Juan knew what he was about to see—the seed of his plan for revenge against TIPCO. The video was a taping of the same variety show he'd been watching, but from a different night. On this episode, an Asian magician was introduced and came onstage. He was dressed in a tuxedo, and from his hands, out of nowhere he produced a white scarf that, upon waving it magically, released a white dove. He was similar to many magicians of the past. What was different this time was that the magician repeated the same move over and over. One time he even simultaneously produced doves of different colors—pink and baby-blue doves that flew away.

By the end of his performance, the Asian magician had

pulled twenty-five to thirty doves from somewhere on his person and released them onto the stage. At the moment when the magician bowed to the audience with a huge smile on his face, Juan's mother came down the stairs and into the little foyer between the breakfast room and the living room.

"*¡Wow, el mago, eh!*" (Wow, this magician, huh!) he said to her.
"*¿Otra vez lo viste?*" (You watched it again?)
"*¿Y?*" (So what?)

Juan told her to wait while he went outside. He walked to the rear patio of the tiny home and climbed the steel rebar stairs up to the roof. The stairs were rungs of metal rebar, installed when the concrete blocks were poured and simply bent in a U-shape, weaving in and out of the wall to create a stair. Rusted and unsafe, they were a ninety-degree climb. Juan made it to the roof and his pigeon aviary, constructed of cheap one-by-three wood and chicken wire. From the roof, he had a view of many identical rooftops, one after another, all holding black plastic water tanks with the word "Rotoplas" printed on them.

The maker of these water cisterns must be a billionaire, thought Juan.

The houses were practically indistinguishable as far as the eye could see. They were so-called Social Interest housing projects, which had improved the lifestyle of millions of former Mexican peasants. The builders had received handsome government grants to build the houses, and they'd done so as cheaply as possible in order to pocket the maximum amount of grant money. Then the buyers began the process of fixing or neglecting, painting or ignoring, until whole neighborhoods became slightly worse or slightly better. Keeping up with the Joneses had helped, but a drug-dealing neighbor had hurt, and this had become a luck-of-the-draw situation for the poor owners of these residences.

Juan opened the makeshift door and entered his large aviary, and the birds became excited. They were racing homers of the finest quality breed, kept by Juan in conditions that were mediocre but safe. He grabbed a small female pigeon and then opened the aviary to allow the rest to fly away on their weekly round. They exited in a flock that circled the area, then flew away to such a distant point that it seemed they were lost forever. He closed the door, because the pigeons would use a Sputnik trap when they returned. Sputnik entrances were simple openings one pigeon-level higher than where food was served in the aviary. Once the pigeons hopped into the aviary, they couldn't fly back out.

Juan came down with a pigeon in one hand. He latched his available hand quickly on each rung, then hopped off the last two, excited to show his mom. Before entering the house, he gently grabbed the pigeon with both of his hands and squeezed it, compressing all its feathers, feeling once again how very small a body these animals had, then tucked it inside his jacket sleeve. Once inside the home, he asked Virginia to sit and watch. He purposefully left the door open, knowing this would drive her crazy, but asked her to bear with him.

While his mother watched from the living room, Juan turned around in the small foyer and made a quick gesture, badly imitating the Asian magician. Juan was a six-foot-tall, handsome young man of barely twenty-five years of age. He wore a blue dinner jacket given to him at his job, and a white shirt and jeans. He let the

15

pigeon out, not like the magician at all. He had to pull the bird out from his sleeve the same way he had placed it inside. When the bird emerged, it was stunned and did not fly. Virginia did not like the presence of the bird in the house, and she winced. Juan moved his hand up and down, prompting the pigeon to jump off his finger and fly out the door safely, out to look for its flock, then he closed the door. The brown pit bull tried to catch the pigeon but failed when the chain stopped it by its neck.

"Terrible!" Virginia criticized.

Juan shrugged and smiled; then they both laughed. Juan went around to the back of the house and turned on the faucet attached to a green garden hose, which he then pulled up to the roof, climbing up the same dangerous stairs while holding it bent tightly to stop most of the water flow. He took advantage of the time the birds were away to conduct the weekly hosing of the aviary. He sprayed water, applying pressure with his thumb on the end of the hose. Water poured onto the roof, and all the excrement floated off the roof and down the gutter. Then he checked all the water bowls, cleaned them, and added water to their reservoirs. The bowls had water that self flowed as its basin drained and lasted for weeks, but Juan liked to add fresh water every week.

Food was a more complex issue. Juan fed the birds daily from a remote opener he had devised. Six bowls had six tops tied to long strings. These strings fed through a piece of garden hose Juan had tied to the roof and strapped to the wood frame of the window in Virginia's bedroom. She pulled one string per day, until the weekend, when Juan would come to refill the bowls. Juan labeled each string with a day of the week. This ceremony took place every week, accompanied with his daily phone call to remind Virginia about the bird feeder and to speak to her briefly. Now, he finished his routine by adding birdseed to the devices from a large container. This was his *pigeon routine*, as he called it, but in reality, it was just one piece of his master plan.

For months, Juan had spent every weekend training his pigeons to return home from increasingly greater distances. He'd read all about how to train pigeons and dedicated himself to the process. He began with tiny baby pigeons, and within a few months, he had a full house. Sometimes training the pigeons would have adverse consequences when one or more didn't return. He'd started with forty pigeons that he'd purchased at almost twenty-five dollars apiece, and now he had thirty-five adult pigeons, fully trained to return home. This pigeon training was the most dedicated and expensive undertaking of his life, and he clashed with Virginia because she had trouble believing he loved birds so much. She was unaware of the motivation behind Juan's actions and for this reason she did not understand them. He told her that pigeons trained like his had sold in England for thousands of dollars, but Virginia just laughed; he knew she thought he was crazy to believe anyone would pay for one of his pigeons.

That evening he didn't talk much more after coming down from the roof, but said good-bye and left, kissing her on the cheek. Virginia was always emotional when he left, so he made short work of the good-byes. She watched him leave in his Toyota Camry that looked beaten and on its last legs. Juan knew that his mom adored him and this reinforced his desire to be a good son.

Juan drove away, as usual thinking about his father

and how Juan remembered feeling great when walking with him and holding his hand. His emotions swelled and he forced them down deep into his body so that the sadness would recede. He turned the stereo full blast listening to rock and tapering his anger. Later on while driving he also had his recurring daydream of the TIPCO skyscraper in Century City collapsing like a Twin Tower...

TWO

Juan hated his work as a breakfast and lunch waiter in
The Savory Yolk, a diner in the Mission Valley area of
San Diego. The restaurant was in a small strip mall on
Friars Road, in a busy intersection between State
Route 163, the financial skyscrapers of Fidelity
Investments, and the freestanding building of the
Quayles Jewels store. He was trained to smile and
serve, and he lived mostly off tips because his salary
was at the legal minimum. His earnings paid for a
room in a house located in the eastern part of Chula
Vista. It was a house full of rooming tenants and he
held no lease. He also could afford to pay for his car,
food, gas and had about nine hundred a month left over
to support his mom. The situation was far from
optimal, and his income barely allowed him any
freedom to go on dates or have much fun. His habit of
paying only the minimum amount due on credit cards
was not helping to reduce the burden.

The long slog of waiter to manager, then to maybe
someday owning a restaurant, was the rags-to-riches
American dream script he was programmed to follow.
Somewhere in the back of his mind, however, he felt
like an outsider, like he didn't fit. The knowledge of

the injustices his father had gone through, and how those had changed his life, galvanized Juan's resolve to find a better way.

On the Mexican side of the border, he bought thin leather and a leather-sewing needle. He also bought beige-colored string for sewing leather strips and snap-on buttons. He went to his mom's and spent weekends there working meticulously, sewing the tiny pouches needed for his idea to succeed. The leather was tough, and Juan learned the value of a thimble. His mother was so happy he was there that she never questioned what he was doing. Each pouch had a carefully sewn snap that easily opened, revealing a small carrying area.

He bought some chicken wire and made a small, impromptu pigeon cage out of the closet in his bedroom on the US side of the border. Every day, he would go to his mom's and visit; then he would stuff two birds into his jacket and cross back into the United States with the concealed pigeons. Sometimes he crossed with four birds, making two trips on the same day. He looked slightly larger, but his jacket took the excess perfectly. The birds always entered a state of panic that caused them to "play dead," and this suited Juan perfectly. In his bedroom, he would leave the TV on so that the bird noises were drowned out and the other tenants in the house would not notice them. He tested his idea by releasing birds from the bedroom window, whereupon they returned safely home to Tijuana.

Juan realized that Virginia was ecstatic that he was visiting her more often, although his sewing probably made the visits seem strange to her. To her way of thinking, this was an activity confined only to women, and he knew she had begun to wonder about his sexuality. One evening, she confronted him.

"*¿Juan, te gusta coser?*" (Do you like to sew?) she asked.
"*No, mamá. Solo que necesito un saco especial para un...*" (No, Mom. It's just that I need a special jacket for a...), Juan replied.

Juan left it at that. He then became extremely guarded and made sure his mom wasn't in on his plans. This was difficult, because she was so nosy. He prepared the suit with thirty-five inner pockets across the front. He then inserted socks from the house into each one to check the appearance. It was hard work. He needed the jacket to disguise the many "balls" created by the socks, and it was so lumpy he began to despair.

Juan wandered the aisles of the open-air markets in Tijuana looking for a solution to the lumpiness in the suit. It came to him when he passed a mattress store. The foam used to make the mattresses was available in really thin sheets, and he inquired as to where he could buy them. As it happened, furniture upholsterers carried this foam product routinely, and he bought a sheet with no problem. He carefully cut the half-inch-thick foam and lined the jacket with it. He found that the suit became stiff and cartoonlike, but disguised the uneven layer of socks inside. Perfect.

Though tired, he began to think about how to accomplish the next and most important element of his plan—the facial disguise. To be successful, his attire and face had to match and could not look in any way Latino. He had ordered a human-hair wig, using a false name and paying with cash. He had to use the cash-advance feature of his credit card, because the wig was expensive as hell. The wig shop was called Secret, which he hoped would be a good omen, and he bought

a blond, male wig of high quality. The wig was fitted
in a way that looked very natural, but being blond, it
then made Juan's complexion look fake. The store
owner noticed and mentioned that he had the matching
skin-tone makeup. After Juan applied it all over his
slightly darker skin, it made him look totally different,
which was exhilarating. He'd never had the experience
of being a blond male, and right away he realized he
would also need to apply the makeup to the backs of
his hands and his forearms. Once he'd done that,
though, he would become someone else! He bought a
pair of inexpensive sunglasses and walked the streets
of San Diego.

He decided to test the disguise on people he knew.
This was risky, because he did not want anyone to
know about his plan. So he proceeded carefully.

Juan entered the McDonald's where he regularly ate
and was taken aback when he reached the cash
register. Pirulin, his regular cashier, looked straight at
him, and Juan almost said hi, but he contained himself.

    "Sir, would you like to try the McRib with curly
fries?" Pirulin asked. "Sir."
    "No." Juan faked a heavy voice.
    "Sir, do you know what you want?"
    "I-I'm sorry, young man, I will not be eating
here."

Juan quickly left, not able to tolerate it much longer,
and heard Pirulin mutter, *"Qué pendejo ese gringo."*
(What an ass, this cracker.)

Juan smiled. The disguise truly worked. He was ready
to move into the major leagues, but he needed to
control his emotions. The minimal encounter with a
casual acquaintance had made his heart race. He

needed to be completely calm. His next move would
be to see how well he could maintain the pretense with
a complete stranger. Juan decided to go to the local
Home Depot and try out the wig. He drove there and
entered the huge establishment. As always, nobody
noticed him or offered to help. He wandered the aisles,
thinking about his plan. He found and grabbed Velcro
tape, carefully reading the length-measurement of the
roll and making a mental note. He would need two or
three rolls, so he carried them with him.

Then he decided to speak to a rep.

"Excuse me?" Juan said. "Do you know where I
can purchase aluminum foil?"
"We only carry radiant barrier insulation," the
Home Depot attendant answered. "It's like aluminum
foil but more expensive."
"I see. Could you show it to me?"
"Follow me."

Juan followed the woman in her orange Home Depot
vest to the insulation section of the store. Once there,
she showed him a cardboard box chock-full of
aluminum-foil tubes that were quilted with perhaps air
inside them. The woman immediately began to walk
away, but Juan wanted to see how much further he
could carry the charade without panicking.

"Excuse me?" Juan said. "Can I ask you
something?"
"Sure. How else can I help you?" she asked.
"I was wondering if you noticed something about
me?"
"What do you mean?"

She began to look at Juan as if it were for the first
time.

23

"If you had to describe me, what would you say?"

"You mean to the police?"

"No, no, just in general. If you went home and your husband asked, 'How was work today?' you would say something like, 'There was this customer that asked me a strange question, and he looked like…'" Juan waited expectantly.

"I see. I would say a nice-looking white man in his twenties, wearing jeans and a long-sleeve shirt under a short-sleeve T-shirt," she described as she studied him, then added, "Thin. Wearing glasses, and with blond hair."

"I just wondered. Thanks," Juan said.

He moved swiftly in the direction of the door, opting for the do-it-yourself checkout stand, where he paid for the Velcro tape, which was not as cheap as he would have liked. His budget was tight, and maybe he could have gotten this on the other side of the border for less, but he decided to save time.

The wig and facial makeup had worked. He took advantage of his disguise to once again go and window-shop at Quayles Jewels. It was always busy, and if one browsed fast enough, salespeople didn't have enough time to approach. And his plan required familiarity with the location.

Later that night, he realized that what was not working was the "thin" comment he'd received form the lady at Home Depot. An image came to him of a movie actor removing his makeup on camera. He needed to find some latex that would make him look fat. This was another step in the right direction and one he could learn from research on the Internet. He needed to appear heavyset, because the jacket made him look heavy, and his face had to match his outfit. There was an added plus to a fat face—when he returned to his normal self, he would be less identifiable. Over the next few days, he studied YouTube videos on the craft of layering latex to enlarge his neck and create a double chin.

A. A. Dober

THREE

The third Saturday of January arrived, and Juan was so nervous he barely slept and couldn't eat breakfast. He had tossed and turned all night, then started his day at 5:00 a.m. He prepared his attire, beginning with his normal clothes, which he would cover with his hand-sewn outfit. He spent an hour applying the latex that gave him the large double chin. The skin color, the prescription-free reading glasses, and the wig completed a look that was in no way similar to his normal appearance. Security cameras would record a picture of a heavyset white male.

The Quayles Jewels store on Friars Road took up an entire city block and catered to middle-income newlyweds. It had a large staff, security personnel, and thousands of jewels inside. Juan entered the store that morning when it opened at eleven, then moved slowly to the rear of the place, looking at displays. He browsed and procrastinated until more customers arrived. Juan wanted a full house for his plan. Within a few minutes, the store was quite lively, and he began his plan by approaching a saleswoman in her thirties.

"Excuse me, do you have larger stones?" Juan asked. "All I see are one- or two-carat rings. I am looking for a larger, single-stone piece."

"We do!" she said with a full smile. "I am Savanna, by the way."

She opened a lower drawer in the case and pulled out a selection of only three rings, each designed with large stones.

"Something like this?" she asked.

"Oh, they are nice." He grabbed one and carefully looked at it, then hummed in disapproval.

"Frankly, Savanna, I am not really looking for a ring. I am looking for a stone to have a pendant made in a design of my own." Juan talked while looking at the ring all the time.
Do you sell unmounted stones?"

"Why yes, but it's the manager that handles that."

"And do they carry large stones? I think three carats is the minimum I want for a pendant."

"Let me call him."

"Thanks."

Savanna went into the manager's office located directly behind her. Inside Juan could see the sofa set with two chairs facing the manager's desk. It was a large and plush office, decorated with maroon carpeting and a tall bookcase set against the rear wall that was full of thick bound books. Bigger deals happened in that office, and newlyweds looking for something a bit more extravagant completed their deal behind closed doors. Savanna returned.

"Our manager would like to meet you." She said. "What is your name?"

"Jay Vogel. Thanks."

She gestured for him to walk through the aisle between the counters, then accompany her into the manager's office.

"Mr. Quayle, this is Mr. Jay Vogel. He is looking for a stone to make a pendant," she said.
"Thanks, Savanna," Elliot Quayle said.

Elliot Quayle was a third-generation owner of the Quayles Jewels store and had been in the business practically from the cradle. He was a good-looking man in his forties, and he had plastered pictures of his very pretty wife and somewhat good-looking kids all over the office. Behind him stood a counter cabinet that housed a safe holding many white-paper packets containing unmounted stones. The inventory was worth tens of millions of dollars wholesale and at a minimum a hundred million retail. The diamonds bought by his father and uncle were never the top of the line but slightly flawed—or three colors removed from—the best stones. All the top-quality diamonds were swiftly bought by the great houses of Tiffany, Cartier, and Harry Winston, to name a few. But Quayles had a good reputation even if it did sell second-tier diamonds. The stones shone beautifully, and most people couldn't tell the difference.

Of course, Quayles also sold zirconia imitations, but those were not handled by Elliot, who was the retail manager for strictly genuine diamonds. Selling an unmounted stone happened rarely but was not unheard of, and for Elliot, the transaction represented an easy profit. Unmounted stones were kept in paper that was labeled in pencil with a handwritten code composed of letters and numbers. The coding system was simple— the purchase price of the stone backward, set between random letters. A stone with the accompanying code "A0B0F2Y8P1" had been purchased for 18,200 dollars. It was a quick way to prevent a mistake and ensure a negotiated price that would include profit.

Of course, the stone was never handed over in the white folded paper, so clients could never figure out the system. The Quayles family had been handling the sale process in this manner since Ely Quayle began trading diamonds in the early 1930s in Los Angeles. He'd had the foresight to move south to San Diego in the fifties, when it was a small and backward city, which Ely had seen as an opportunity to be on top.

In the first meeting, Elliot stood up and shook Juan's hand. He failed to notice that Juan's hand was thin and strong, which did not match his pudgy face.

"I am told you are looking for a rather large stone," Elliot said.

"About three carats," Juan said in perfect English. "Not too large."

"You are aware of the cost of such stones? I don't mean to insult; I am merely trying to make you aware that such stones are rare and costly."

"How much are we talking about?"

"For three carats, they start at around forty-five or fifty and go up to eighty depending on their quality."

"That is not a problem."

"You would have to pay with secure funds, so a check or wire transfer is usually best for these transactions, and you cannot take possession until after the money has cleared our bank. Are you OK with this?"

"Clearly. But first I must be enamored of the stone."

"Absolutely! I am sure we have what you are looking for. Let me see, three-carat pieces…"

Elliot slid open the door on the wooden buffet cabinet

that stood beneath the window. The window was wired with alarm trim that dated back to the 1970s but was left on by the Quayles as a visible alarm deterrent. There were no bars on the window, and Juan could see the grass behind the building, and beyond, a concrete sidewalk. Palm trees and beautiful gardening surrounded the store—a pretty view to have from one's office.

Behind the cabinet door was a heavy steel safe that was installed there before the cabinet was built around it. It was made by the European firm Adlersafe, and Elliot opened it by simply turning the lever. It was kept in the open position of the combination until the end of the day. He pulled out a black velvet drawer that was labeled "2.5, 3, 3.5" on its front edge and held many square-folded envelopes. He turned around to find Juan closing the office door and walking back to the desk.

"You don't mind if we have some privacy," Juan said, hoping Elliot did not notice he had turned the lock on the doorknob.

"Of course, of course," Elliot said as he unfolded a white paper envelope and showed Juan a beautiful, large square-cut stone.

"That is magnificent! Do you have a loupe?"

"Yes."

Elliot looked in the drawer to his right and removed a jeweler's loupe. During this distraction, Juan put on a pair of cheap green latex gloves he had in his front jacket pocket, where he kept a thick plastic cable tie. Elliot found the loupe and turned to face Juan but instead he saw the large black gun aimed at his forehead. His face turned into a whiter white as blood rushed inside his body, making his head light and his heart palpitate at great speed. Juan was pointing a

Glock 9 directly at Elliot's forehead.

"Now don't do anything stupid," Juan said.
"I won't."

Elliot instinctively placed his foot on the floor buzzer
hidden below the carpet that activated a silent alarm.
He pressed down on the switch.

FOUR

Inside the Western Division police precinct in the
Mission Valley area of San Diego, a bulletin board
listed the highlights of the day. Most investigations
related to drug operations, another handful to petty
crime. That Saturday, the majority of the precinct's
officers were out on patrol, and the only pair of
detectives still working at the precinct were Ivory
Godwit and Cliff Gold. Of these two, Ivory was
trained locally by the academy back in the early years
of the first decade of the new century, and she had
seen her fair share of crime. Cliff had moved to San
Diego from New York and never looked back. The
precincts there were dirty and constantly full of
perpetrators. The difference in quality of life in San
Diego was enormous, and his wife was so happy.
Initially the move brought problems and feelings of
regret, particularly involving being so far from family,
but adjusting to San Diego was easy—no hurricanes,
no snowstorms, no traffic, no noise at night, a real
backyard, miles of beautiful canyons to hike…the
pluses added up. But for all the California healthy
living, Cliff's genetics prevailed: he developed the
same body he would have had he stayed back in
Brooklyn. Too many carbohydrates plus beer made for

a large stomach and flaccid overall body. Being a detective didn't help, because there were no physical requirements. He still had a heavy New York accent, even though it had been sixteen years since he'd relocated.

They heard the buzzer of the silent alarm and immediately looked at their computers, identifying it as the alarm for Quayles Jewels. The usually closed door to the captain's office swung open and Captain Brent Argus looked around.

"Cliff and Ivory, go to Quayles Jewels and see what's up," Brent ordered. "It is a silent alarm but we are calling all cars. Hurry and report back to me."

"Yes, sir," Cliff said, grabbing his car keys and badge.

Cliff always took off his badge while at his desk; it bothered his ever-growing waistline. And turning fifty was not helping his metabolism, either. He looked at Ivory, and his look was encouraging her to hurry up. Ivory was not off her butt yet, but stood immediately upon seeing his gaze.

"Come on, Ivory, somebody could be in danger!" Brent urged.

"I just know it's a false alarm again," Ivory said.

"Well, let's hope so," Cliff said.

With that, they left the office to speed off to Quayles in their unmarked black Chrysler 300. The precinct office had a Gaines Street address, but most of it was actually on Friars Road, the same road on which Quayles was located. Exactly eight minutes away.

"This is not what I was expecting this morning," Ivory said.

"Yep. Me either." Cliff responded. "You think this is a holdup?"

"I am not sure. It's kind of early to go about robbing a jewelry store."

"Now that you say that...It is rare." Cliff swirled past slow cars.

Cliff drove fast—but not too fast—and from the moment the silent alarm hit the precinct to their arrival at Quayles Jewels would take exactly ten minutes. Ivory hated Cliff's driving and, come to think of it, the driving of all of her former partners, as well. Cliff drove slow and steady and nothing like a California driver. Ivory was a native and drove fast, and always above the speed limit as if her time was too precious to waste inside a car. Her speeding was probably genetic, or simply a factor of the large distances between places in spread-out San Diego. She was the baby of three siblings in a home with no police ancestry. Both her mother and father disagreed with her career choice, but sometime in her early childhood, maybe while watching *Law and Order*, she had made up her mind. She would not allow anyone to take her dream away from her.

When they arrived at the store, Ivory could see that there were no signs of panic outside.

"Obviously no one is aware inside that there is trouble. Or it is a false alarm. Head into the parking lot and let's go in," Ivory said.

"Roger that," Cliff said.

The car pulled up to the sidewalk, but before making the left turn into the parking area, they both heard a familiar noise coming from a distance that unsettled them. A police siren was approaching. Ivory snapped the radio immediately.

"This is 2-A-13, this is 2-A-13, Central come in," Ivory said into the radio.

"This is Central, come in 13." The speaker was male.

"We requested a 211S on the Quayles Jewels approach. A patrol is fast approaching with a siren!"

"On that."

Ivory couldn't believe that some rookie would mess the approach. They moved slowly into the parking lot, driving around back to the main door to the huge jewelry store. The Quayles building was a two-story structure that looked like a very tall single-story building because of its surrounding double-height column structure. The brick columns reached high up, transforming into arches, and stood on three sides of the building, leaving the fourth side for an outdoor, open-air hallway. The parking wrapped around the back and side, and the store's two facades sported business logos that faced Friars and Frazee roads. The building was impressive for an independent jewelry store. No suspicious vehicle or people were visible outside the store's perimeter, and customers were exiting calmly, making Ivory and Cliff feel the alarm might have been false.

"All cars, all cars approaching Friars Road, 211, please turn off your sirens!" The male voice broadcast loudly from their radio. "This is code S. I repeat, code S. No sirens."

The siren stopped. And then they could see the police car arrive at the lot, going fast. Ivory was so angry she leapt out of her car, flashed her badge at the rookies, then approached them, tapping on their window.

"Thanks for ruining a silent approach," she said. "Please move your vehicle to that spot there and wait until we call for backup. This might be a false alarm, and until we assess the situation, just back off and stay vigilant. My partner and I are going in."

"Yes, ma'am," the officer said.

The police car backed up onto the side of the parking service road. Ivory walked back and motioned Cliff to join her. About eighty feet from the front door, Ivory stopped Cliff to assess the situation and make a plan.

At that moment the two main doors of the Quayles Jewels store swung open and many frenzied pigeons flew at great speeds out of the store, followed and surrounded by a handful of customers in shock and awe. Feathers hung in the air after the birds disappeared into the sky. They moved at high speed to the left of Ivory and Cliff, then turned immediately south. One or two birds almost hit Ivory, and she ducked. They moved erratically and fluttered coming out of the building. The people all moved slowly toward their cars, and neither Ivory, Cliff, nor the uniformed officers later recalled seeing the blond man in a dark suit who walked directly away from the entry doors and through the hedge that divided the Quayles parking area from the adjacent office building.

"What in the world!" Ivory said.

"Geeez!"

Cuco, the Mexican-American security guard, came out moving his hands around and shaking off feathers. He was at the entry door where all thirty-four pigeons had funneled out and was the victim of the most feathers.

"Let's go in," Ivory said as she sprinted to the open front door.

Cuco walked back inside, and he was polite as Ivory walked in. He was cluelessly unaware that she was a cop and thought her a new client. The remaining patrons and the staff inside were stunned and surprised at having had so many birds in the building. Everyone was shocked and talking about what had just happened. Cuco had opened the doors to let customers out and to allow the pigeons to exit, because the birds had seemed afraid.

"What happened?" Ivory asked him, flashing her badge.

"I don't know, suddenly the store was full of pigeons and customers began to scream, and so I opened the door to let them out. They flew away and now you come in? Is there a problem, officer?" The armed guard asked.

"Close these doors and don't let anyone out. Understood?" Ivory commanded.

Cliff closed the doors and the guard helped him.

"Lock them. Is there another way out?" Cliff asked the guard.

"Only in the rear, but it is alarmed," the guard replied. "So it must be closed."

"Stay here; we will need to take statements from everybody," Cliff said.

Ivory went to the back of the store and found Savanna trying to open the manager's office, which was closed firmly. She moved the doorknob but the door was shut.

"What is it?" Cliff asked Ivory loudly from across the store.

"It's a 211 in progress! Go out there and get help from those officers; you need to stop everyone who left the building! Now!"

Cliff was a bit shocked by being ordered around by Ivory, but she was right. He ran immediately for the front door and crashed into it. The guard had locked it.

"Open this door."
"But…"
"Just open it!"

The guard opened it.

"Now, don't let anybody out. Capisce?"
"Huh?"
"Only let police in and out, nobody else. OK?"
"OK."

Cliff screamed at the two officers and looked around. He saw a couple starting their car and backing up to leave. He ran at them screaming. "Police, stop. Police, stop!"

They kept going but needed to stop before merging into Friars Road, where they would be gone for good. Cliff ran and became winded almost immediately as they merged into traffic. He took his cell phone out and clicked an image of the car and its plates as a last resort. Another car was behind him trying to get out onto Friars Road and Cliff was blocking it. He did not move to address the driver from the side, fearing he would drive off. He took out his revolver, pointed it at the driver, and screamed at him to get out of the car.

Meanwhile, Ivory pushed at the closed office door. She could feel something heavy was blocking it. Behind her were the floor manager, a man in his forties, and Savanna. Not being able to open the door, Ivory turned to Savanna.

"What happened?" Ivory asked.

"The pigeons flew all over the store and we all were shocked and looking at them. They flew all around until Cuco, the door guard, opened the doors and they flew out. It was a spectacle!" Savanna said.

Ivory looked at her as if this information were useless.

"They all flew out of here," the manager said.

"And you are?" Ivory said.

"I am Robert White, the manager. The floor manager."

"Do me a favor, Bob, and see if you can push this door open."

"OK."

As Bob pushed hard the door began to budge a little. It wasn't locked but a heavy object was blocking it. When it revealed about a half inch of space Bob peeked inside and could see that it was a chair. He pushed again.

"N-noooo."

The muffled grunt with a clear *no* was heard, now that the door was open.

"Mr. Quayle, is that you?" Bob asked.

"Mmm-hmm," Elliot responded from behind the door.

"If I keep pushing, maybe I can help?"

"N-noo."

"Why, what is it? Are the other people in there with you?" Ivory questioned.

"Mmm-hmm," Elliot answered, his voice still muffled.

"This is 13 calling Central, we need backup. Yes,

40

SWAT. Over," Ivory spoke on her radio and then turned to the floor. "Everybody back up! Clear this area now!"

Ivory moved everybody back behind the counters and she assumed the position with her gun behind the counter for cover. The door to Elliot's office was now a dangerous site.

"Everybody to the other side of the store."

Savanna and Bob moved to the south side of the store where all the people were. Cliff entered, having left the other two officers outside with the three customers they'd stopped from leaving. The situation was escalated to a "211 in progress," with the perpetrators still inside. He touched his Kevlar vest beneath his shirt just to make sure it was there. He held his gun up, and all the customers and staff watched him as he moved past them toward the rear and the manager's office. He looked at the people as they stared at him and realized the situation was far from optimal.

"Everybody get down, on your bellies," Cliff ordered.
"You can't keep us in here," a man said.
"Yes, let us out. What if they start shooting!" a woman cried.

Cliff decided to opt for the safety of what could become more hostages. He looked at Ivory and motioned for her to keep an eye on the manager's door. Then he faced the group of people. At a distance, sirens converged, and he knew he could handle this.

"Everybody, we are going to exit the store and go to the parking lot on the left. Nobody, nobody is to run or try to escape. You are all considered suspects at this

point, and I need your patience and cooperation.
Understood?" Cliff said.

They all nodded. Cliff looked at the guard and
motioned for him to open the door. He did, and a
dozen people left the building, including Savanna and
Bob White as well as all the customers and the rest of
the employees. Cuco the guard also left, and Cliff used
him to help with the crowd. Outside, the three other
customers and the policemen stood looking at them.

"Get police tape and make an area to hold these
people. We need to clear them before they can go
home. Start by taking their information, and make sure
you see ID—don't just take their word for it. Any one
of these people could be a suspect. Capisce?" Cliff
ordered.
"Yes, sir."

Just then about six officers arrived at the same time.
Some with weapons drawn.

"We will wait for the SWAT team. I need you to
hold these people here in a safe area and secure the
perimeter. You two go to the rear and make sure
nobody leaves the building. Keep an eye an all doors
and windows. If you need more officers, get them."

Cliff then entered the building and went to his
partner's side. The front doors to the Quayles store
were left open.

FIVE
Ten minutes earlier…

Juan was in Elliot Quayle's office, staring down the barrel of the airsoft plastic gun that resembled a Glock 9 only because he had spray-painted it. Elliot looked genuinely scared, but that had not prevented him from calling the silent alarm. Juan was unaware that he would have only ten minutes before the police arrived, but moved fast.

"Close your eyes and don't say a word, or it will be your last. Keep your hands where I can see them," Juan said coolly, not raising his voice.

Elliot did so and Juan moved around his back and pulled a previously curled black zip tie from his jacket pocket.

"Now slowly move your hands behind your seat."

Juan placed the plastic gun on the rear counter without making any noise, and then swiftly tied Elliot's hands. He swiveled the chair so Elliot would face the rear wall of the office. From his other jacket pocket, he pulled a white silk scarf not unlike a magician's scarf

43

and gently pushed it into Elliot's mouth. Then he pushed him toward the wall on the rolling chair to clear the area of the desk. Elliot was silent and Juan turned immediately to his new task.

He began by quickly taking the first pigeon out of his jacket and held its leg tightly with his left hand. He grabbed the first stone Elliot had shown him and placed it in the pouch of this bird. He pulled another folded paper square with a diamond from the pile of folded papers on top of the tray Elliot had placed on the desk. He grabbed the diamond with two fingers and dropped it carefully into the same pouch and repeated the procedure a third time. He wanted the load to be light and manageable for the bird. He knew they could handle even more weight, but it was better to err on the low side. Then he clicked the clasp to close the pouch using both hands and released the animal. It flew immediately to a nearby couch. Elliot was startled by this. He turned his head and stared at the pigeon. Juan did not care about Elliot anymore. He had limited time and needed to move fast. He took another pigeon out and pulled a folded paper square with another stone from the pile on top of the tray. He opened it with a single hand and placed the stone into the pouch. Twice more, then clicked it. Again.

Sometimes there were two smaller stones in an envelope, and he would place the two into the pouch. He was averaging fifteen seconds per bird. He was fast. Ten, then twenty, then thirty, and finally, the last five birds. He heard a distant police siren, and there was knocking on the door.

"One moment!" Juan said amicably.

By this time, Elliot was aware that most of his two-and-a-half- to three-and-a-half-carat diamond inventory was in pouches on the birds. He had seen the small artifacts close up, because he was sitting with a bird on his shoulder, one on his head, and the one in front of him on the bookcase, that was staring at him. By now the purring and fluttering of the birds was becoming loud, and hence the knocking. Obviously Savanna was wondering what the noise coming from the office was.

The instant Juan filled the last pouch he walked to the door, removed the latex glove on his left hand and then his right, and opened the door with the plastic gloves as if they were a towel. He placed them in his pocket and walked out. The birds started to shoot out on their mission to reach their home and Juan walked normally, surrounded by shooting birds that flew straight through the main floor toward the front door circling the showroom. Cuco the guard stood there as birds flew all over and customers screamed. A couple was walking to the door and wanted to exit as birds passed near the guard and, in desperation for the pigeons' predicament, he opened the left door as a customer pushed the right door open. Juan walked directly out without rushing, heading straight for the hedge not thirty feet from the front doors. Another customer who was ready to leave did so at that time as well. In total four people left the building at the same time as the birds. The birds provided a perfect distraction. He walked calmly through the parking lot of the adjacent building fully aware that the video cameras in all building parking lots would be evaluated. He knew this heavyset white male was visible going to and from the store on foot. The property behind Quayles Jewels was a simple office building with no exit onto Friars Road. It, too, had cameras on the parking lot. This property led to a cul-de-sac that exited onto Mission Center Road.

Juan continued to follow Mission Center Road, turning

left away from the jewelry emporium and toward a highway overpass. As he entered the overpass he looked to make sure no cars were coming, then took off his jacket and felt the cool San Diego air dry his sweat. He arrived at a large tin barrel used by homeless people to generate heat. He pushed the jacket into the barrel and then removed his elegant black pants with a tug. They were taped together by Velcro at the side seams and revealed his jeans beneath. Then he peeled off the jaws of latex that gave him his heavyset look and removed the wig. His shirt also came off, as well as his sweaty T-shirt underneath, exposing him further to the cold. Before chucking the shirt into the bin, he used it to remove the whitish makeup from his face as best as possible, while all the time making sure the area under the overpass was empty.

A soda bottle filled a third of the way with a clear liquid sat beside the metal drum, and he picked it up and emptied the container over the clothing and wig. He took a book of matches from his jeans pocket and threw a lighted match into the barrel, then immediately crossed the street to his parked Camry, which was facing north on Mission Center Road. Inside the car he looked in the mirror and finished cleaning the makeup from his face. He started the car and drove one block north to Westside Drive, made a right, then parked in the first empty spot on the street he could find. Then he walked back into the strip mall, to begin his regular job at the Savory Yolk restaurant. He entered from the rear and sat on a stool in front of the employee lockers and all the delivery boxes. He put on his employee shirt and removed all the sweat on his body, washed his face in a sink, then was ready to start work. He was late by a half hour for his work and knew that any minute someone would walk in and see him back there. He sat on the stool and leaned on the lockers, pretending to be asleep. His mind reeled and his heart finally began to calm down. His blood pressure was pumping madly, and now that the theft had worked, his body switched from fear to happiness! He had no evidence on him and his loot was flying across the border to his Tijuana home roof. He couldn't wait to see it. For now, he just sat there, pretending he was sleeping and giving the impression that he had arrived there earlier.

"Juan!" Finch, the manager, yelled.

"Oh, what? Hi?" Juan answered.

"How long have you been there sleeping?"

"Not long."

"Don't lie. Did you clock in?"

"Oh, shit, I forgot." Juan said as he approached the point-of-sale computer to clock in.

"Good! At least we are not paying you to sleep."

"Sorry, it's just that I had a crazy Friday and slept little."

"Do you want to go home? You tired?" Finch was being cynical.

"No man, I really need the money."

"Then get to work and stop slacking."

Across the street, patrol cars converged and a helicopter hovered over the Quayles building. Juan began his routine of setting tables and only occasionally looked over. His manager and the other employees were talking about the action across the highway and began to channel-surf on the TV, looking for the local news.

"A breaking news story is happening at the famous Quayles engagement-ring store on Friars Road. We have Tori Taka reporting from the scene. Tori, what do we know right now?" The anchor on the Channel 7 News asked a pretty Asian-American woman in her late twenties who stood on the grass a good fifty yards away from the store. The whole storefront of Quayles could be appreciated in the shot. Behind her the police had closed the area, and various police trucks were at the scene. Finch called everyone to come and see. There were no customers yet.

"Thank you, Chip. I am standing here at the Quayles Jewels store and we have exclusive information that a gang of thieves is inside the store, holding it up at gunpoint. Customers were taken hostage, and the SWAT team has arrived. It is a developing story and one that could turn ugly at any moment," Tori said.

"Tori? How many thieves? How many hostages?" Chip asked after hearing the questions in his earpiece, something reporters from smaller cities don't know how to fake.

"Chip, I am told that the majority of the customers and employees have been evacuated to safety. I have been informed that only one hostage is inside in the manager's office. We have reason to believe that it is a member of the Quayles family but have no confirmation. It is up to SWAT now. These are very tense and critical moments."

Juan looked at the screen, listening, but continued to work. He was delighted by the lack of information on the news. The fact that they still thought the thieves were in the building was perfect.

"Finch! Finch!" Juan called.

"What?" Finch asked.

"Look at the helicopter, man! Can you believe the thieves are still in there? There is a hostage and all."

"Yeah, I heard, man. What do you care? Go back to work."

"Just saying. I mean, nothing ever happens here." Juan spoke to Finch as Finch walked away, dismissing him.

Juan had established that the thieves were across the street, so if Finch were ever asked about him, it would provide a perfect alibi.

A. A. Dober

SIX

Minutes earlier as Juan left the jewelry store, Elliot had stood up on his legs and with the chair on his back, he made his way as fast as he could toward the door and pushed it closed before the last bird left. He reacted instinctively in an attempt to stop the diamonds from leaving. A single pigeon was still in his office when he closed the door in a haphazard move that ended with his fall. His body and the chair lay sideways, keeping the door closed. Elliot then stared at the one pigeon inside the room. He also noticed the Glock 9 gun on the console behind his desk and the many papers all over the floor that once housed precious stones. Many, many of these diamonds had left, flying away. Who would believe that? This bird was proof of what happened and the only clue to who had done this.

A thought occurred to him. *They could follow the bird back to the thieves' lair.* His mind reeled as people began to push on the door. He needed to prevent them from entering because the bird would fly away!

"Nnnnnoooo."

Elliot worked his tongue muscles, trying hard to push out the silk scarf. He finally managed to remove the scarf by pressing his mouth to the floor and having the friction of the rug tug at the scarf. Little by little it came out until he pushed it out with the help of his diaphragm, which he filled with air. *Pawgh*—a final cork-popping kind of sound he made.

"Hello!" Elliot screamed.

"Hello, this is Detective Godwit. Who are you?"

"I am Elliot Quayle."

"Who is there with you?"

"No one."

"What? Let us in, then."

"Please listen. I am blocking the door, do not open it. There is a pigeon in here with a pouch filled with diamonds strapped to its leg. If you open the door it will fly away with them. They are worth tens of thousands of dollars!"

"What?" Ivory was shocked. "But I saw many pigeons leave the building, dozens."

"The thief put diamonds on each and every one of them. I saw him do it. He tied my hands to the chair. Then they flew out. Are any still in the shop?"

"No. The guard opened the doors to let them out."

"Damn it!" Elliot said.

"Cliff, call off SWAT. We need an animal handler. A net," Ivory commanded as she stood next to the door Elliot was behind. "And make sure the front door is closed, just in case the last bird escapes from the office. And check that all windows are closed."

"Roger that," Cliff responded and walked over to the front doors to lock them. He used his walkie-talkie to stand down the SWAT team. From behind the glass, he could see a barrage of officers in black, pointing guns at him.

"Mr. Quayle, I am going to push the door open just a little to see in there. The front door is closed."

"No need, I can move." Elliot moved a bit away from the door. "Here."

With that Elliot allowed Ivory to peek. She saw the bird on the desk inching to leave. It made strange purring sounds and kept looking at the gap in the door. She could see Elliot's hands and the zip cord.

"Mr. Quayle, please scoot over to the door gap. I think I can cut the straps on your hands if you just get over here."
"OK, good idea."

Elliot scooted and squirmed to where the one-inch gap allowed Ivory to access the zip cord. She turned around and looked for scissors. None were nearby.

"Do you know where they keep the scissors?"
"There are none on the floor. We don't allow them. Don't you have a knife?"

She looked to the back where Cliff was talking into a walkie-talkie, stopping the SWAT team's assault on the building.

"Cliff, I need a pair of scissors or a knife. ASAP!" Ivory commanded.

Cliff opened the doors and was immediately rushed by the senior SWAT commander.

"We need a pair of scissors. The building is empty except the manager. Stand down."
"We still need to enter. It is our job. The perimeter must be secured, and every inch of the building must be cleared."
"OK, but I need scissors or a knife right now. Anyone have a knife?"

Immediately all the SWAT members pulled large black knives from their sides. Cliff grabbed the one closest to him, which was the commander's.

"Nobody come in yet. Until I call you."

He ran back into the store, only to immediately turn back and explain. "Oh, yes. We must keep this door closed until we secure the bird inside. There is a pigeon carrying diamonds, so he must not fly away!"

Cliff arrived and gave Ivory the SWAT team commander's huge, sharp black hunter's knife.

"Mr. Quayle, don't move. I am going to cut the plastic."
"Call me Elliot," he said.
"OK, Elliot. Don't move."

Ivory cut the hard plastic, and it was easier than she expected because the knife was so sharp.

"There."
"Thanks."

Elliot stood up and closed the door.

"I'll kill that bird!" Elliot said.
"Don't! Don't!" Ivory screamed.
"I won't, I'm just mad. I know we need it. We can follow it back to the thief."
"The thief! Was it a single person?"
"I don't know, but I only saw the one."
"How did he bring so many birds into the store."
Ivory kept up the conversation through the closed door. It was awkward.
"Let me catch the bird first and then we can talk,"

Elliot said.

Inside he approached the bird but well before he could get near it flew on top of the bookcase cabinet opposite the door. Elliot was powerless sooner than he thought.

"Motherfucker!" Elliot screamed.

"What happened?" Ivory asked.

"He flew to the cabinet top. I can't reach it there, and he is too fast. We need a net."

"Wait a second." Ivory said and immediately called dispatch and spoke into the walkie-talkie. "Thirteen, come in. What is the ETA on the animal handler? Bird animal handler. Over."

At that moment the door opened and Elliot Quayle came out fast and closed the door immediately behind him. The bird was trapped inside, but he wasn't anymore.

"Whew!" He said.

"Hi, I'm Detective Godwit." Ivory introduced herself.

"Hi, Elliot Quayle. I've just been robbed! By a bunch of birds! I guess you got the silent alarm. Did you catch the fat bastard!"

"No. We do have everyone who was in the store when the pigeons were released, though. So the perpetrator is here," Ivory said.

"Good," Elliot said immediately.

"Cliff, do you mind staying here and ensuring the bird doesn't fly away?" Ivory asked. "Make sure they don't harm the bird, because we need to follow it back to where the others went."

"Ivory. Can we talk?" Cliff motioned to speak to her in private.

"What is it?" She whispered.

"One car with two passengers drove off."

"What, so we don't have everybody?"

"No, but I have the license plate."

"OK, stay here but call the plates in and identify the vehicle. Maybe you can get in touch with the owners, and if they are innocent they can come back to be cleared."

"OK, I'll watch the door. You might as well send the SWAT guys in, just so they can leave sooner."

"Will do." Ivory walked back to where Elliot stood.

"Mr. Quayle, let's go."

"Elliot, please."

"Yes, sorry, Elliot. Let's go."

Ivory went to the front doors and spoke to the SWAT team outside with Elliot by her side. Reporters were beginning to arrive, but she motioned for them to stay away.

"Commander, I know you need to enter," Ivory said. "We believe the building is empty, but you are welcome to do your assessment provided you do not enter the manager's office. There is a pigeon there that has diamonds on its leg. In a pouch. It is a homing pigeon trained to return to its home. We cannot lose this bird. You understand? We are waiting for animal control to arrive."

Ivory saw Captain Brent Argus arrive in his unmarked vehicle. She made a beeline for him.

"Sir. We have a bird…" Ivory started.

In a few minutes Brent was informed.

"We will wait for animal control," Brent said.

"This is Elliot Quayle. He was the hostage. Elliot, this is Captain Argus." Ivory introduced them.

"Nice to meet you," Brent said. "I am sorry for the circumstances."

"Not your fault," Elliot responded. "I am glad you are here."

"We have the perpetrator in custody. I am bringing Mr. Quayle to look at all the people that were in the store at the time. This way, we can release the innocent employees and customers."

"You mean you got a good look at him?" Brent asked Elliot.

"Absolutely. He wasn't wearing a mask or anything," Elliot said.

"Let's go." Brent rushed them.

They moved to the grassy area where thirty or so people sat, stood, and moaned in aggravation, surrounded by police officers and yellow plastic crime-scene tape. Behind them were reporters' vehicles and the back of Tori Taka with the Yummy Yolk sign across the street. Elliot walked up and down, looking at everyone who stood there. The perpetrator was clearly not among them.

"He's not here," Elliot said.

"But everyone is accounted for," Ivory said.

"Are you one hundred percent sure?" Brent asked Ivory.

"Well, not one hundred percent; two got away. But Cliff is tracking the license plates now. Let me call him," Ivory said and began to dial Cliff on his cell phone.

"If all we have is license plates, you know what that means!" Brent looked furious.

"Cliff, any luck on the license plates?" Ivory asked, putting Cliff on speaker phone.

"The car belongs to a couple who live in Tierra Santa," Cliff said. "They just got home, and I spoke to both of them. They are on their way back, to be identified and cleared."

Brent did not look happy.

"We have the bird, right?" Elliot asked, sensing
that there was not much hope in the air.
"Animal control should be arriving any minute,"
Ivory said.
"I would like to go straight to the security footage.
Who here is your IT guy, Elliot?" Brent asked.

Elliot glanced around for Peng, his trusted Chinese-
American head of security.

"Has anyone seen Peng?" Elliot asked.
"No. He was not in today," Rob the manager said.
"That's not good," Ivory muttered.
"Rob, please call him at home and let me speak to
him. Do you have his number on your cell?" Elliot
asked.
"I do, sir."

Rob called Peng and put the phone on speaker.

"Peng, is that you?" Rob asked.
"Yes," Peng spoke to Rob.
"Mr. Quayle is here with me he wants to speak to
you." Rob said.
"Peng, could you come immediately?" Elliot
asked.
"But it's my day off," Peng said.
"It is of the utmost importance that you come here
now," Elliot said.
"What happened?"
"We've been robbed."
"I'm on my way."

Rob hung up and Elliot looked at Ivory.

"You heard him; he is on his way in," Elliot said.

"Good. Let's go look at it," Brent said.

"Are we going to wait for Peng?" Elliot asked.

"No." Brent cut him off and went to the inside of the store.

"Sir, what do we do with these people?" Ivory asked.

"Everybody stays until I see the tape. Understood?"

"Hey! We want to go home." Several people shifted restlessly, complaining.

Brent did not stop and left Ivory to deal with the crowd. Elliot followed Brent.

"Everyone stays. You heard the Captain, unless you want to remain a suspect in grand theft, which is a serious felony," Ivory said loudly.

"Oh..." The moaning continued, but was muted.

"What a hassle," someone said.

"The inspector will view the security footage, and you will all be in the clear soon. Bear with us a little longer," Ivory said.

The crowd settled and became calm. The bird in captivity was calm as well.

SEVEN

Back at the Savory Yolk restaurant, Juan kept working, but he purposefully did everything slow and wrong. He knew his manager would get upset with this behavior as soon as customers arrived. He pretended to slur words and moved with a dizzy walk.

"Juan, what's gotten into you today?" Finch asked.

"I am not feeling well," Juan said. "I might be catching something."

"You were sleeping on the job, back there."

"I know. I dozed off, but I hadn't clocked in. I am just not myself today. I feel fatigued."

"Just help me through the start of the lunch hour. At least till one."

"OK, I'll try."

Juan knew Finch was really lazy and relied on the staff to do all the manual labor. Once the tables were set and people got their drinks and entrées, most of the hard work was done. But today, he needed all the time he could get. By now the birds were probably at his mom's, and he needed to get back as soon as possible. He kept going until he saw the perfect opportunity. A

customer came in, and he recognized her. She was a
regular who was fastidious about cleanliness; almost
every time she ate here, she returned glasses and
cutlery, asking for cleaner ones.

"Hi, Juanito," she said.
"Hello, Mrs. Fregata. Nice to see you today.
Where would you like to sit?" Juan asked.
"I'll sit over there by the window."
"Perfect."

Juan pulled out her chair, and as she sat, he sneezed all
over her and the table.

"Hey! Cover your mouth, Juan!" she screamed.
"Sorry!" Juan said.

She stood up and made a beeline for the ladies' room.

"Now I need to wash off the germs. Please change
all the plates and silverware on my table, the glasses,
too. Disgusting!"
"I am so sorry," Finch said. "Juan, clean it up."
"Not him! He has a cold. Can't you see? God.
People need to learn not to work when they are sick,"
she said.
"You are right, Mrs. Fregata. Juan, go home. You
are too sick to work today. Clock out and leave."
"Yes, sir."

Juan left, clocking out at the register and grabbing his
stuff from the locker. He was out the back door in less
than sixty seconds. He drove to the house to clean up
all the bird-related items in his room. There were bird
feathers to remove, and the cage he had made of
chicken wire over the closet door. He vacuumed, then
emptied the dirt inside the vacuum into a plastic bag.
Then he packed his few belongings in a suitcase and

left with the rolled-up chicken wire in his car. He drove down a side street in Chula Vista, shaking the garbage bag out the window of the car while driving with one hand. Feathers and dust flew down the street, the wind carrying them in every direction. Then a few blocks to the south near J Street, he threw the chicken wire into an empty lot. Nobody saw him. It would be untraceable and would probably disintegrate into rust within a few years.

Juan drove down Interstate 5, south to the border as fast as possible. Absolutely no trace of what had transpired at Quayles remained in his car. The border crossing is usually easy going south, because there is no US inspection on the American side going to Mexico. In Mexico there is an inspection, but it works on a lottery where a green light is a pass or a red light is inspection, and it is completely random. Returning at three in the afternoon meant little or no line of cars waiting to enter Mexico.

At the border Juan noticed that there were cars waiting. And he also saw that everyone was getting a red light. As he crossed the speed bumps with his red light he hooked a right to pass further inspection. American officers were working with the Mexican officers on the Mexican side; it was the first time he'd seen this. They stopped each car and looked inside every trunk, and inspected underneath the cars with golf-like poles adapted with small mirrors. Juan suspected they were trying to stop the thief of Quayles Jewels, but he could not be sure.

    "¿Qué pasa?" (What's up?) he asked a Mexican guard.
    "Nada. ¿Tu tranquilo no traes nada ilegal?" (Nothing; stay calm; are you bringing anything illegal?) the guard said.

"Nada." (Nothing.)
"Sal del auto." (Get out of the car.)

Juan got out of the car. Evidently the guard was not sharing information. The American officers went into his car and looked all over. They opened his suitcase and found only clothes and toiletries. They cleared it.

"Ya te puedes ir." (You can leave now.)
"Gracias," Juan said, thinking, *Thanks for nothing.*

Juan left, a bit rattled but safe. He drove straight to his mother's home, said hello to his mom, and climbed up to the aviary. There he found the birds had reentered the aviary using the Sputnik trap on the side as they always did. The birds cooed and ate the food left for them the night before. His first instinct was to remove the stones. He grabbed a bucket and began one by one grabbing a bird and removing the pouch with the stones. He counted each sack as he went. Thirty-four. Thirty-four. He counted the sacks and looked for the last bird in the pack. It was hard. There were nooks and crannies and shelves and divisions in the aviary that made it hard to find the final bird.

He was reluctant to take the next step. He was attached to these birds and they had performed their job remarkably well. They had moved the stones across the border, complicating the law enforcement efforts of the Americans. But now he had no choice. His bucket had thirty-four sacks with a fortune in diamonds. At retail, they represented a good ten million dollars, which would be the number Elliot Quayle would try to recover from TIPCO. If they were sold at high discount, Juan would have returned to his family the money owed to them by TIPCO. *Justice delayed, but not denied,* he thought, having heard this

adage in a documentary on the Holocaust that he had
seen on TV.

He went downstairs and found some heavy-duty black
plastic garbage bags. He came back upstairs and sat at
the door of the aviary, wringing the necks of the birds,
one by one. In about five minutes, there was complete
silence. He cried. Tears fell down his cheeks in an
unexpected flow of relief, revenge, sorrow, success,
and fear that was uncontrollable. The birds all fell into
the black bags. Thirty-four birds. Then he looked
everywhere. He confirmed his fear; one bird was
missing! What did that mean?

EIGHT

Brent, Ivory, Cliff, and Elliot sat in the IT room at Quayles Jewels, watching the security videos rewind in slow speed. They were powerless to speed up the technology that stared all four in the face.

"Can't you speed it up?" Brent demanded.

"I don't know how," Cliff said. "I've tried."

"So you don't know where the fat man got the pigeons?" Ivory asked Elliot.

"It must have been a bag, but I swear he had nothing on him. He was just a man in a suit. It was like magic," Elliot explained, because he had not seen where the birds had come from.

"And they were so many!" Ivory said.

"You saw them?" Brent said.

"Yes, we did," Cliff said.

"Many, many birds. It must a have been two dozen or more," Ivory said.

"Two dozen. Where did they come from? Could the perp have placed them inside your store ahead of time?" Brent asked.

"I don't think so. No. Impossible," Cliff said.

"Why not?" Brent asked him.

"They make too much noise," Cliff said.

"I see. The staff would have heard them even before opening," Brent said.

"Exactly. What I'd like to know is where are the pigeons going?" Elliot said.

"Tell me something, Elliot, how much do the diamonds weigh?" Brent said.

"The largest stones he took are three-and-a-half carats, and they weight three-quarters of a gram!" Elliot said.

"So we can see how much weight the bird was going to move by examining the pouch of the one in the room," Ivory said.

"Where are we on the handler?" Brent asked.

"I'll check," Ivory said and left.

"Cliff, call IT at the precinct and find out what the smallest battery-operated GPS weighs," Brent said.

"It sure needs to be small if we are to have the bird carry it," Cliff said.

"Get the answer and don't waste time with the obvious, Cliff!" Brent scolded.

"Yes, sir, I'm on it," Cliff said.

Ivory came back with Peng, and Savanna followed, all walking into the room. Elliot was happy with the idea of placing a GPS tracking device on the bird. And overall, with Brent now taking the lead, he sure appeared to know what to do.

"The animal is safely in the handler's birdcage, and she removed the bag from the bird's ankle," Ivory said, handing the little pouch to Elliot.

Elliot snapped open the clasp on the small rectangular bag with a folding top. Four large diamonds were inside. Cliff returned, having called the IT department at the precinct.

"Look," Elliot said. "Four, which weigh about

three grams."

"Peng, right? Can you speed this tape back?" Brent asked Peng.

"Easy," Peng said and clicked twice on the Rewind icon.

The DVR started to rewind at four times its normal speed. Peng double-clicked again, and it increased to eight times, then sixteen times. In a jiffy, they got to the portion of the tape that had recorded the chaos of the birds on the floor of the store.

"Stop there!" Brent said.

It took them a few minutes to go through the crime. A single, blond heavyset man entered the store, walking in from the parking lot after having crossed through the hedges. He hadn't parked in the lot, and when he walked past the cameras, he never looked up—he always had his head angled down. He wore glasses, and they watched him interact with Savanna at the counter, then enter Elliot's office.

Then Cliff came back. "Twelve grams!" he interrupted, as if his information were foremost on everyone's mind.

"What?" Brent retorted, annoyed, as he kept watching the cameras.

"Twelve grams is the weight of the smallest GPS IT can get hold of. It is solar powered. No batteries, and it's about the size of a quarter."

"Mr. Quayle, can you weigh the leather sack and the stones?" Brent asked.

"Savanna, bring me my scale," Elliot said.

"Yep, coming up." Savanna was happy to play a role.

The tape now showed how the heavyset thief entered Elliot's office and a few moments later the door closed. The cameras showed the store was operating normally, and no one looked suspicious.

"You have no camera in your office?" Brent asked Elliot.

"No," Elliot drily answered.

"Peng, please fast-forward through this part, up to the point where the perp opens this door," Brent said.

Peng did it.

"There!" Brent said.

They all stared at the camera, trying to see the perp's face. The fat man walked straight to the front door looking down and ignoring the show. All the other people were looking at the birds fly about desperately, trying to get out. The man left right when Cuco opened the door, and on the outside camera angle they watched as he walked straight through the hedges.

"Did you notice that?...Ivory, you didn't see this guy," Brent said.

"I must have, but I thought they were two couples. See, it's four people leaving," Ivory explained.

On camera they could see Ivory and Cliff enter the store less than a minute after the perp left.

"Did you notice the difference?" Brent said.

"I didn't notice the man," Ivory said. "I'm sorry."

"I didn't notice him either, sir," Cliff said, supporting Ivory.

"I'm not talking about that. Peng, can you go back to where the perp walked in the first time. Now everyone look at him here, when he's leaving. Now show us when he enters," Brent commanded gently.

Peng had been taking notes on a pad. Almost instantly, he was back at the time 11:01 where the crime started. They all looked at the man walking in.

"Same guy," Cliff said.

"Yes, stupid. Not that!" Brent admonished. Elliot and Ivory laughed, but Peng was too serious for laughter.

"He's fatter," Ivory noticed.

"Exactly," Brent chimed.

"He is also walking much faster leaving than coming," Elliot said.

"You realize that he is not holding any stolen goods!" Ivory said. "Even if we stop him now, he won't have any evidence on him. How can we prove he is the criminal?"

"Cliff, get access to the camera in the adjacent building, and see where he goes after he crossed this hedge. Maybe he parked there, and we can get a plate. Also, instruct them that we will need copies of all the tapes they have. As far back as possible. This guy must have cased the joint. And cordon off where he crossed, and look carefully there. We might get a footprint, torn fabric, etc....Take forensics with you and seal that area. Also, get forensics to examine the feathers, maybe they can discover something we don't know about these birds."

A police officer arrived.

"Captain, we found the perp's gun in the office. It's a toy," the officer said, handing over a Ziploc bag containing the black spray-painted toy gun.

"Thank you. I need you to go outside and release all the people who have given their statements. The perp is not among them, but we can't rule out an accomplice," Brent said, grabbing the toy gun as he instructed the officer.

"Yes, sir. Got it," the officer responded and left.

Meanwhile, Savanna was plugging in the jeweler's electric scale on the desk next to Peng.

"I feel so stupid," Elliot said.

"Don't," Brent said. "You couldn't have known it was a fake. You were right to cooperate. Period."

"Thanks," Elliot said, then saw Savanna with her what-are-you-waiting-for look, prompting him to weigh the sack and stones on the scale.

"Peng. I want copies of these tapes made immediately. I want my team to look at them more closely," Brent said, turning to him.

"Will you provide the necessary subpoena?" Peng asked.

"We will," Brent said.

The scale displayed "7.31963" in digitally lit red letters.

"Just over 7.3 grams," Elliot announced.

"That is 4.7 grams less than the GPS the officer mentioned," Peng said.

"Thanks for the math, Peng," Brent said. "What we need to know is, can the bird handle twelve grams, and can we get the GPS in time?"

"In time?" Elliot asked.

"Well, I don't expect the thieves will sit with the birds and the loot and wait for us. Do you?" Brent said.

"You got me there. So if this bird leads to the thief's home, he could be gone from there by now?" Elliot asked.

"Maybe. I would. I expect people in the vicinity have seen the birds, and once the news reports this, they might put two and two together. I really doubt the thieves will stay near the pigeon coop."

"Aviary," Peng said.

"What?"

"Pigeon aviary, not coop. A coop is for chickens."

"Thank you, Peng. Aviary. Motherfucking aviary," Brent said the last line very quietly, but they all heard it.

"Sir, I just Googled how much weight a homing pigeon can carry, and they say here they can handle up to 2.5 ounces," Ivory said. "But I don't know how many grams that is."

"That is...about...70 grams," Peng said.

"What are you, a computer?" Ivory asked.

"Seventy grams, hmm." Brent thought out loud.

"That is enough for the GPS," Elliot said.

"Yes, but why would the thief only load up each bird with seven grams when he could have sent seventy?" Brent said.

"Well, it says here that they can carry up to seventy on their backs, with training," Ivory said. "This pigeon was carrying its pouch on the leg, though. And perhaps with no training."

"Still, either he didn't know, or there is a reason," Brent speculated.

"What if the distance the pigeons were to travel was great, and the thief wanted to be sure the pigeons would make it? It makes sense to send them light," Peng said, feeling like a detective.

"Good thinking," Ivory said.

"Thank you," Peng shyly said, gazing at Ivory as if she were the last woman on earth.

Ivory felt a bit creeped out by the silence that ensued. Finally Brent spoke, breaking the awkward vibes she was getting from Peng. "Ivory, take this to forensics and see if we can get a print." Brent handed the gun to Ivory.

"You won't," Elliot said.

"Come again?" Brent asked, annoyed.

"He wore latex gloves," Elliot said. "He put them

on while I looked for a loupe."

"Do it anyway, Ivory, and see where that toy came from, where it was made. I want the full story on the weapon," Brent said. "Capisce?"

"On it," Ivory said, then left.

"You are a thorough man, Captain," Elliot said.

"I am also done here. Peng, prepare our copy of the footage as soon as you can. How many months do you have of archived tapes?" Brent asked as he stood up.

"Six," Elliot replied.

"Well, I want my people to view them all. Like I said, the perp had to have cased the store. Ivory and Cliff are lead on this; I will have Cliff come to pick them up when he has time."

"Can you send Ivory?" Peng asked, then regretted having said anything at all.

"I'll just pretend I didn't hear that," Brent said. He picked up the pigeon's leather harness that had held the diamond pouch, put it in his jacket pocket, and left the IT room.

He walked to the office of the manager and looked around. The bird was still in there, in a cage. The handler was gone, and there was no one from forensics. He looked for Yonit, his favorite forensic expert, but didn't see her anywhere.

NINE

Cliff walked with Adler, the uniformed officer who was helping him, across the parking lot of the building adjacent to Quayles Jewels. Ivory and Cliff were being sent on different lines of investigation by Brent, so now Cliff had to deal with a newbie officer. Tori Taka of Channel 7 News followed them, making no effort to be quiet about it.

"Cliff! Cliff!" she yelled.

He looked back and saw her, then stopped to talk to Adler before she was close enough to hear him.

"It's fucking Tori Taka. You go on and find out if we can access the footage from that camera." Cliff told Adler, pointing at the camera mounted over the stoop of the office building.
"OK, boss. She sure is hot," Adler said.
"Go on, and keep those comments to yourself."
"Sure, boss."
"Didn't you go to harassment training?"
"Sorry, boss, she didn't hear me."
"Still. Now go."

Tori caught up to Cliff.

"Cliff, thanks for stopping. What is the scoop?" Tori asked.

"Hi, Tori. No scoop yet," Cliff said.

"Aw, come on. Please give me something. I have nothing, zip."

"I almost got caught last time. If I'm seen here with you, it will not further my career. I need an incentive."

"Listen, there is this company party at Petco Park, happening during and after the baseball game, and I can get you tickets. You can come with your wife and kids. Some of the players will be there to sign autographs. Would you like that?"

"That sounds nice."

"Tell me something I can use."

"OK, but if you don't come through with those tickets…"

"Relax."

"It was a single thief. Get this: he left without the loot."

"He escaped, but didn't take anything?"

"He did escape, but he didn't take the loot."

"What?"

"We don't know how he did it, but he managed to get dozens of pigeons into the store, and then released them carrying diamonds in tiny sacks."

Tori listened in amazement. She was dumbstruck, but not enough to quell her investigative reporter instincts. "How do you know this?" she asked.

"I saw the birds leave, and there are countless witnesses. The store was filled with birds and feathers…" Cliff stopped himself; he needed not to divulge the capture of the one bird.

"Wow, how much was stolen?"

"We don't know that yet."

"Was there a getaway car waiting for him?"

"Tori, I've said a lot. You owe me. Capisce?"

"OK."

"Now go away. I need to get back to work."

"One last question. Did you see the tiny sacks on the birds?"

"They were homing pigeons. They used to carry messages in the old days. We believe they carried the diamonds."

"Flying diamonds!"

"I need to go. Bye."

Tori watched him head toward the adjacent building, and she couldn't imagine why. She immediately dialed her phone.

"Jonah, are you there?" Tori spoke into her phone as she walked back to Quayles and her news truck.

"Yes, hold on." Jonah was the chief producer at Channel 7 News, and he called the shots. After giving someone instructions, he came back on the line. "Give me something."

"The thief stole diamonds. Get this…"

"Thief. So there was only one."

"Yes, a single thief, and listen. He put the diamonds on pigeons and released them! They flew out the door to who knows where, carrying the diamonds! And get this, he got away. Even if they do catch him, he has no evidence on him! It is all flying through the air."

"That's the scoop. Stay there and find out more details. Interview anyone who saw the birds. This is going to be our lead, Tori. Good job."

Jonah hung up and immediately popped his head above everyone in the news production area.

"Everybody! Attention! We need to get footage of

flying pigeons coming out of the Quayles Jewels store this morning at 11:00 a.m. Go to adjacent buildings and get the footage. There must be something we can use," Jonah announced.

"Why flying pigeons?" a staff member wondered out loud.

"The pigeons were homing pigeons, and they flew back to their home. So presumably, they went to the thief's home. They were carrying the stolen diamonds. Everyone start calling, look at Google Maps, and see where there can be footage of this. Now!"

The entire newsroom was surprised with the information. It would only take about a half day before they were flooded with footage. One piece came from a Scripps Hospital building on the south side of Mission Valley, high up on the hillside and facing north. This footage showed a speck of dark matter coming out of a tiny building on the other side of the valley that grew and grew until it became a discernible flock of pigeons, and they passed right in front of the camera as they flew south. The video was so clear you could count the birds. Jonah had the perfect image for the six, seven, nine, and ten o'clock news. This image was of the actual birds, flying from the scene of the crime and carrying millions of dollars in diamonds!

TEN

Panic set into Juan's bones as he recounted the sacks. *Thirty-four. Thirty-fucking-four,* he thought.

If they had a bird, they could trace the animal back to the aviary. He didn't know how, exactly, but it was a possibility. And all those gringos on the Mexican side of the border meant that the Mexican authorities were cooperating. Paranoia set in, and the only thing he could do was to move fast. Do everything in his plan, but faster.

"Ma...Ma!" Juan raised his voice.
"*¿Qué pasa?*" (What is happening?) Virginia asked.
"*¡Te tengo una sorpresota!*" (I have a huge surprise!)
"*¿Qué mi hijo?*" (What is it, my son?)
"*Te acuerdas que querias ir al DF y que no teniamos lana para ir?*" (Remember you wanted to go to Mexico City but we couldn't afford it?)
"*Sí.*"
"*Pues mira. Nos vamos al DF. Sí, no hoy en la tarde, mañana en la mañana. ¿OK?*"

(Look, we go to Mexico City if not this afternoon, tomorrow morning, OK?)

"OK."

"Así que empaca pero a la de ujule." (So go and pack, and do it quickly.)

"Pero…" (But…)

"¿No empiezes a cuestionar, quieres ir o no?" (Don't start asking questions. Are you coming, or staying?) Juan threatened.

"Voy." (Coming.) Virginia agreed.

"Andale a empacar." (Go and pack.)

Juan returned to the roof. His plan called for removing the aviary and totally obliterating the evidence, but now he was wondering whether removal of the aviary was such a great idea. If the bird came back, it would have to be flying on its own. So unless they had a helicopter following a pigeon, there would have to be a GPS on the bird. Was this even possible? He decided to keep the aviary but dispose of everything else and be prepared so if the thirty-fifth bird showed up, he could kill it, take the GPS and destroy it, and then quickly dispose of the aviary.

Juan dumped the bird bodies and the leather straps in a metal drum like the one under the overpass where he had burned the clothes. He doused it in kerosene and threw a match. He went to the freezer, removed the ice from the ice trays, filled them with water again and dumped the stones in the water. Then he placed the trays back in the freezer. In a few hours, he would have ice cubes worth millions. But this was a perfect place for now. Virginia never used ice, and they were invisible in case they were robbed. Right before leaving with his mom on the trip to Mexico City, he would put all the ice in a thermos bottle. It would be visible the entire time, and the clinking noise the diamonds made would go unnoticed, since they would sound like ice cubes.

He went up to the roof and began a thorough cleansing of the entire floor and aviary, using Clorox and picking up everything down to the last feather. He left a single tray with food and some water for the last bird. He brainstormed how to know when the bird arrived. It could come in through the Sputnik trap at any time and would be followed by police. The safest thing to do was to act immediately, right when the bird arrived. If the bird never made it back, then it would be safe to stay in this home.

As long as the bird existed, he couldn't know for certain when it would come back, and this made the home unsafe. He needed to completely disappear. Fortunately, he now had the resources to do that; they just somehow needed to be converted into cash.

"Ma…Ma!" Juan screamed.

"*¿Qué?*" (What?) Virginia answered, poking her head out the window.

"*Has tu maleta pero igual no salimos hoy. Tal vez mañana no se. Nos llevamos todo porque no le voy a pagar renta a Buitre, quien sabe cuanto tiempo nos vayamos.*" (Pack your suitcase, but maybe we won't travel today. Maybe tomorrow, I am not sure. And pack everything because I don't intend to pay rent to Buitre, who knows how long we will be gone.)

"*¡Qué contrariedad!*" (What a hassle!) Virginia said.

Juan felt compelled to stay up on the roof. It was hard to leave the area, because the arriving pigeon needed to be immediately checked out. The smell of charred pigeon meat permeated the air, and there was a crude resemblance to chicken. He felt a pang of hunger in his stomach.

I need to know when the bird arrives, without having to be up here. I need an alarm! Juan thought. His panic shut down any creative thinking, and he just sat there, staring into the distance, with close to ten million dollars in diamonds in the refrigerator of his tiny home in Tijuana. He sat there, feeling simultaneously empty, insecure, and victorious. It was not what he had expected to feel. If only all the birds had made it home, he could already have taken down the aviary and left for Mexico City. He planned to drive in his Camry with his mom. He already had eyes on a high-end jeweler in Mexico City, to whom he planned to sell the first diamond, so that he could begin his new life. His plan would allow his mom to live in complete luxury in the metropolitan city she had grown up in and loved. The missing pigeon was a complication of huge proportions.

ELEVEN

Brent stood in Elliot's office, wearing disposable booties and blue latex gloves, and looking for anything that might give him a clue as to the thief's state of mind. As he looked around the desk, he detected the behind of a beautiful woman crouched on all fours under the desk. Just the one he was looking for.

Yonit was an Israeli woman with a decade of forensic experience. Brent liked her not only for her experience, but also for her good looks. He preferred Yonit over all the other forensic personnel, because she was fast, direct, and had no political correctness, which cracked him up.

"Yonit. This is a welcome surprise," Brent said, gazing at her behind.

"Stop staring at my ass, Brent." Yonit retorted. "And don't come around, you are contaminating the scene."

"What happened to 'Hello, Brent'?"

"Give me a second. I thought I had something here, but it is nothing. You know these office cleaning crews are not very thorough; down here, it seems as if

it has never been vacuumed. Yuck!" Yonit exclaimed
in her endearing accent as she crawled out and shook
her head in a friendly gesture toward Brent. She wore a
white jumpsuit and the same booties and gloves as he
had on.

"Hi."

"Hi."

"Anything?" Brent asked.

"Perhaps. First, there are no strange residues or
footprints of any kind. We have feathers, many pigeon
feathers, *Columba livia domestica* to be precise, but
other than the species, there is nothing else they can
tell us." Yonit pointed to the pigeon in the cage.

"Hmm."

"From what I can tell, the perp didn't touch
anything with his hands. He was super smart. Not your
average thief. No fingerprints anywhere."

"But we are going to catch him. We have him on
tape."

"I did find something that might be an important
clue. But you are not going to like
this."

"What is it?"

"A hair."

"From the thief's head? How do you know it is
from his head?"

"It was on top of these papers here, you see."

"So?"

"Well, these are the wrappers of the diamonds that
he stole, and the hair was on top of them, so it stands
to reason that it fell after or during the robbery."

"You have the one hair? That is good."

"Yes, the one. Not good."

"What? It's blond, right?"

"Yes, blond. But get this, it was a dead person's
blond hair, no root, and where the root should have
been there were traces of rubbery glue, particularly
cyanoacrylate adhesive, so it's the human hair of a

wig."

"So my video is of a disguised man. Damn it! Fuck!"

Brent was not happy; he immediately took out his phone and called it in.

"Paloma, it's me. Call off the search for a blond man. He was wearing a wig, so remove 'blond' from the description, but keep it a white male, six feet, heavyset, and do it now."

During this, Yonit kept working. She heard the conversation and felt bad for what she was about to say. Smeared white cream was apparent on the white diamond wrapping paper she examined on her portable microscope.

"You are not going to like this," Yonit said.

"Now what?" Brent asked, hanging the phone.

"There appears to be some kind of makeup material on the paper. The perp probably touched his face with the latex gloves at some point, who knows, then he smeared it on these papers. It is in most of them, so definitely it was on him before."

"Can we get DNA from it."

"Very unlikely. It is a makeup cream, not a substance that will scratch cells off the skin. I will look for some." Yonit looked at him and noticed he finally got what she was saying.

"So he is not white."

"Exactly. Probably not heavyset either."

"So what we have is a six-foot-tall man."

"He's a smart one."

"I'll catch him."

Sure, Yonit thought, but kept quiet. This was looking like a perfect crime.

"Cliff, where are we on the GPS?" Brent left the message on Cliff's phone as he looked at the bird. The pigeon looked at him and then turned its head.

He glanced around, and saw some of his police men standing by. One stood nearby the door of the office where Brent and Yonit were.

"Hey, get me the animal handler," Brent commanded.
"Yes, sir." The officer left.

Brent took the leather contraption out of his pocket and handed it to Yonit. She looked at it for the first time.

"Anything on this?" Brent showed it to Yonit.

She looked at it in detail. Examined the clasp device, the string used to make it, and the leather. Meanwhile Brent sat on the sofa, looking at her. There were feathers everywhere and he avoided some pigeon feces that sat squarely on the other side of the sofa.

"Well?" Brent pushed.
"Nothing," Yonit said flatly.
"Nothing? Really?"
"It is suede, quite common, the string is cotton, also quite common, and the clasps are manufactured by the millions and sold in any sewing store, generic really. So it is a handmade harness for a pigeon. Nothing in it can lead to a particular person."
"OK, hand it back. I need it."

Yonit threw it to him and he moved to catch it but winced at the feces all around him. She continued working on the microscope and the room. Then a small, thin woman arrived, probably about twenty-seven years of age, and perky, reminding Brent of the people who work at SeaWorld.

"Hi. I am the bird handler," she said.

"Please have this leather harness that you removed put back on the bird. Without letting it escape, of course," Brent commanded.

Brent handed the harness to her. She immediately began the procedure by closing the door. Brent looked on as the two women did their jobs. He dialed again. "Cliff?"

"Yes, sir?" Cliff answered.

"Why didn't you answer before?"

"I didn't get a call; did you call? What is it?"

"I need an update on the GPS."

"IT is going to bring it to the scene. I am looking at the footage from the office building, but I will call and get an ETA? OK?"

"Do that, and, Cliff? Anything on the video over there?"

"Yes, the perp walked across the parking lot, but did not get in any car—he just walked off down the sidewalk and into Mission Center Court. Didn't even run. In the footage we can see some of the birds in the distance, but they went in the opposite direction. One bird sort of strayed into the parking lot, but then it turned to go meet the others."

"Is there a camera beyond that point?"

"That is where we are heading now—in Mission Center Court."

"OK, good work. Get copies of all the footage sent to HQ. Keep after him, tracking him building by building. We need to see his car or something that can identify him!"

Yonit was packing up; he watched as she placed the microscope back in its case. The bird handler was finished, as well.

"That will be all, thank you," Brent told the
handler.

"Thanks; this is so exciting," she said.

"Oh, Miss, please do not tell anyone what is going
on here. You need to keep quiet." Brent pressed his
finger to his lips. "The news cannot alert the perp that
we have his bird. Capisce?"

"Sure. I won't discuss this. How long, though?"
she asked.

"Until I tell you. You cannot share any
information with anyone. Not a thing."

"OK."

She left.

"She will Instagram the entire crime scene before
the day is over," Yonit said as soon as the handler was
far enough away. Brent laughed.

"I just hate this Internet society we live in. It is
impossible to keep anything from the media.
Anything," Brent said without knowing that, thanks to
Cliff, by nightfall the news would have the birds on
camera leaving the scene, accompanied by the
headline "Flying Diamonds!"

TWELVE

Ivory arrived at headquarters to assess the plastic toy gun and to determine whether it had any prints on it. She went to the forensic lab to meet Roderick Anser, a massively built Nordic individual who had a tendency to leer at women. Ivory, for one, was creeped out by him, although he did not mean any harm. He was like a huge teddy bear who looked ghoulish, but for those who knew him, it was quite funny. Ivory had left with the second-most important piece of evidence in the crime after the bird. Yonit could have dusted for prints, but if there was a print, the database was here. Finding clues about the gun itself was not something that could be done out in the field.

She found Roderick leaning over a table, peering at tiny specks of dust and using tweezers to carefully place them on glass microscope slides. "Roderick, can you tell me if there are any prints on this?" Ivory asked.

"Can it wait? I am busy." Roderick answered, stopping and turning toward her.

"I have a Code One, issued directly by Detective Sergeant Argus."

"Hand it over." Roderick put on a fresh pair of latex gloves.

Ivory gave him the large zipped plastic bag containing the toy gun. She kept quiet about what Elliot had said. There was always a possibility of finding a print that the perp had made before he used the gloves. Roderick handled the gun carefully, placing it under a large loupe on a swivel base and moving it under the glass. He gazed at it, then whistled.

"What is it?" Ivory asked.
"Clean as a whistle!" he replied.
"You are not funny."
"No, I mean it. There is nothing here. I don't even have to dust it. There is no grease of any kind," Roderick said as he changed the light to a blue light.
"So nothing?"
"It is cleaner than Mr. Clean himself."
"Thanks. Can I get it back?"
"Sure."

Roderick put it back inside the bag.

"You know anything about that type of toy? Or the paint used to make it black?" Ivory asked.
"Hmm, let me see…It is an airsoft gun, very popular with teens. It used to have a red front, you see?" Roderick said as he scratched the black paint from the plastic tip of the toy, revealing the red beneath.
"So it was a red toy."
"No, not all of it, just the tip. See here. But the perp covered the entire thing with matte-black paint." Roderick scratched the gun on the shaft, revealing a shiny black beneath the matte-black layer.
"I see. Is there anything else you can tell me?"
"Not really. It is a common toy, spray-painted

with a common paint. Hard to place."

"Thanks!"

"Not a problem. Anytime." Roderick went back to his other analysis.

"Really? You are not the least bit curious about this case?"

"Nope."

"Well, it is the most exciting case I have ever been on!"

"Hmm."

"Really."

"OK, what is the case about?"

"A guy stole millions of dollars in diamonds, and guess how he got them out of the jewelry store?"

"Hmm. At gunpoint?"

"No. Guess again."

"In a toy car? He got away in a toy helicopter? On a toy boat?"

Ivory was growing irritated, so she just blurted it out. "He placed the diamonds on homing pigeons and released them!"

"What? But how did he get the pigeons into the store? I don't believe you."

"I saw the birds leaving! It was amazing! I think it was a perfect crime. Even if we catch the guy, he is clean, not even the gun in his hands, let alone the diamonds."

"Smart. And where are the diamonds?"

"Back at their home, wherever that is."

"It could be in another country."

Ivory looked at him and immediately realized that what he said was probably true. "You are kind of a genius aren't you?" she asked.

"Hmm." Roderick flushed from an unexpected compliment.

Ivory left and called Brent on her cell. She walked the hallways of the precinct, ignoring everything except

the ringing on the other end. While she waited for
Brent to pick up, she stopped at a coffee machine and
made herself a cup of coffee.

"Brent? Ivory here."

"Yes, Ivory. Report," Brent said.

"Elliot was right. The gun is clean as a whistle. No
prints. It is also very common."

"That totally sucks."

"Yes, I know. Also, I was speaking with Roderick,
and he mentioned that the pigeon idea was brilliant.
But get this, he asked me what country the pigeons
were flying to. Get it? In the old days, these pigeons
sent messages between countries in Europe. So these
pigeons could be halfway into Mexico by now."

"I thought of that; it is the logical plan. But if this
perp thinks for one second that we will be stopped by
the border, he is sorely mistaken. Anything else?"

"No, sir. Dead end."

"Go to Quayles and start scanning the footages for
the past several weeks for any suspicious person
casing the joint. Especially people moving near or into
Elliot's office. The IT guy there will be happy to help
you."

"Yes, sir. Understood."

Brent was surrounded by three tech guys all looking
and arguing about the bird and the GPS. One of them
kept referring to the batteries in the GPS.

"I thought the GPS was solar powered?" Brent
asked all three techies.

"That was a prototype—impossible to get hold
of," one of them answered.

The conversation moved to the biggest hurdle,
following it at pigeon speed. A helicopter was selected
as the best possible mode of following the GPS. The

logistics were awful, and it would need approval from higher up the chain of command. Before Brent called the police chief, he finished the task at hand. "Excuse me! Guys, what happens if the batteries die in the GPS?"

Some of the guys were about to start laughing when a brave techie looked at them, then explained. "Captain. The batteries will send the GPS signal every minute. It is like a short burst of information detected by cellular towers and then relayed to the base. We get the information and see a blue dot like this." The tech guy showed an iPad with a map and a blinking GPS.

"Just like my phone," Brent said.

"Exactly. Now what happens if you run out of batteries in your cell phone?"

"I see, that is not exactly what my question was. I know it sounded stupid. What I meant was, is the GPS fully charged, and how long will the batteries last?"

"That is more like it. It is fully charged, and 24 to 48 hours."

"Why so little?"

"Because it is so light."

"I see."

"When can the pigeon be released?"

"When you tell us. We are ready."

"Good. I will get the helicopter here, and we can start the mission."

As much as he hated having to ask her for anything, Brent called the police chief.

"Police Chief Sadana's Office." Gaby, the police chief's secretary said.

"May I speak to her, Gaby?" Brent asked.

"Captain Argus, right?" Gaby asked.

"Yes, it's me. Again."

"What is it this time?"

"I need the helicopter."

"I'll put her on."

Brent waited, listening to pleasant music while on hold. It was an old Natalie Merchant song, but he barely paid attention to the lyrics.

"Brent. What is this about the helicopter? Are you nuts?" Police Chief Jarita Sadana said.

"No. I really need it this time."

"It already left your area," she shot from the hip.

"I can hear it—it's still hovering nearby!"

"It is needed elsewhere. You guys lost the perp, even though he supposedly left when you arrived. So you passed him in the hallway, and he winked at you and disappeared. Sounds like one of your girlfriends."

"Very funny. Ha, ha. I am laughing, really. Now how about a helicopter ride to TJ? Coming with me?"

"You know we can't just fly into Mexico unannounced. What are you talking about? Is it this bird story? Explain."

Brent and Jarita had been partners until she decided to play politics and moved up the food chain. Brent held her in high regard, and vice versa. He quickly explained the entire crime to the chief and detailed the logistics of following the pigeon to the thief's lair. Also the timeliness of the issue. She immediately changed her tune.

"Brent, call it in. Hop on the helicopter and pursue. I will alert the mayor so he can speak to the authorities in Tijuana. That is where you think the birds went? Right?"

"It is a guess. I mean, it is the nearest point across the border, but the bird could be flying back to Guadalajara for all we know!"

"So if the bird goes farther than the helicopter's tank of gas we are done?"

"Yes and no. We can still send people on to the arrival location. But we would lose the element of surprise. There is also…"

"What?"

"The bird could go to a place where we can't land."

"What do you mean?"

"Well, what if the bird goes into a forest? We will know it is there, but that is it."

"The element of surprise is already lost by what, four hours?"

"Well, we needed to assess the situation, then find a GPS that a bird could fly with. We weren't twiddling our thumbs!"

"OK."

"Is that a yes?"

"Just do it."

"Thanks.

"And Brent?"

"What?"

"Good luck."

"Thanks, Jarita, I'll need it."

Brent hung up and called the chopper to land on the lawn in front of Quayles Jewels. He then proceeded to choose which techie to take on the ride. The nice techie that showed the iPad to him was the obvious choice.

"What is your name?" Brent asked.

"Dick."

"Are you ready?"

"For what?"

"You and your tracker are coming with me on the chopper. We will follow the bird to the thief's lair."

"But-but…"

"No buts."

"I don't even have my passport. You said we are going to Mexico," Dick asked, looking concerned.

"Relax. First, we don't know if we are going to

Mexico. Second, you are a police officer—you are under the purview of this operation, and if we do go into Mexico, you will be on a list of known officers. OK?"

"Grow a pair," a second techie muttered.

"Yeah, R, don't be a wuss," the third techie interjected and chuckled.

"OK, I'll go. But I hate flying," Dick said.

"Have you flown in a helicopter before?" Brent asked.

"No."

"Then you don't know the meaning of the word hate. Let's go!"

Brent called Cliff at that moment. "Cliff. Report."

"Sir, the video on the adjoining buildings followed him down Mission Center Road until he just walks off. From that point there is an underpass and he went in that direction. When we got under there, we found a steel drum smoldering, really stinky. He probably burned his hairpiece there, because it smelled like burned hair. We had no water to stop it, so we turned it over and kicked at the flames to try and salvage some evidence. I called Yonit to come and see if she can get anything from there. It is all carbon-looking to me. No sign of the perp. On the other side of the underpass, there are no video cameras until way up a hill. I will go there next and see if there is a shot that of him exiting from the underpass."

"It sounds like a dead end. He could have had a car parked there. Look for evidence of a car that was parked recently, maybe a fresh oil leak. Listen, who is there with you? Is he good? Does he understand what we need next?"

"I think so…" Cliff said, looking at Adler across the street swatting a bee as if it were an invisible monster.

"Send him on to the next cameras; I need you

back here immediately. We are going on the chase."

"Yes, sir, right away!" Cliff sounded excited.

It was like a ceremony. The parked helicopter, the police cars running, and all eyes on a small birdcage being carried by Brent and placed on the roof of a police car. Cliff arrived at a run and was ready to pilot his car on the chase.

"I will get in the chopper and hover on the other side of Friars Road. The chopper is on channel 123.050, so tune your radio to that frequency, so that you can hear me." Brent instructed. "I will give you the command to release the bird, and you follow behind. Don't worry if we go faster, because we will be calling ahead to police in that direction. Hopefully, when the bird lands we will be right behind it. OK? Capisce? Like you say?"

"Yes, I'll wait till you hover on that side of Friars Road. Got it. And it's pronounced capisce!" Cliff said, using the Italian pronunciation of the American slang.

The commotion drew Ivory out of the tedious and impossible job she was undertaking. Finding the thief as he cased the jewelry store without any idea of his looks was impossible. Almost two-thirds of all the visitors to the store were single men looking at rings, deciding, and pricing for an engagement. Many never bought a thing. It could be any one of thousands. So when she saw Brent leaving with the bird she followed.

The helicopter took off as soon as Brent got in. Dick sat next to him, looking a bit pale and immediately changing to very pale. The movement of the chopper was not what Dick expected—it was not a forward movement like a plane but arbitrarily up, down, right, and left, and he held on to whatever he could grasp. Including Brent's hand, which he clutched like a child in desperate need of his father.

Brent smiled as he put on his headphones. "Can you hear me, Dick?" Brent said.

"Yes! I hear you!" Dick blasted the speakers.

"No need to scream, son. We can hear you. Now, didn't I tell you that you would hate it?"

"I do."

"You can let go of my hand, now. Can you see the bird on your screen?"

Dick let go and clicked the iPad on. The blue dot was right on the map where Cliff was parked, and there was a red arrow indicating the iPad's location. The red arrow and the blue dot almost touched each other.

"Yes, sir."

"Cliff, are you there?"

"Yes, sir, copy loud and clear," Cliff spoke through his radio on the same frequency.

"All systems go."

"Copy that. Bird on the loose. Fly away, feathered friend!" Cliff opened the cage door.

"Save your snappy comments, Cliff," Brent said.

"No, sir, it's not a snappy comment. The bird is not leaving the cage."

"Well don't talk to it, man! Make him leave the cage. That is an order."

Cliff clumsily shook the cage, and that was enough to make the bird flap madly, giving Cliff a scare, whereby he clumsily dropped the empty cage and shook around in disgust at the bird feathers on him. Officers nearby laughed but pretended to be serious as he turned, looking to see who had laughed.

"Very funny," he uttered under his breath, looking defiant.

The bird flew out and away, in the direction of Tijuana just like his feathered friends had about four hours earlier. From the chopper, it was a tiny grayish dot shimmering in the sky. Ivory jumped into the shotgun seat of Cliff's car.

"I don't think you are supposed to be here," Cliff said.

"You have no idea what I was doing. Pointless and impossible," Ivory said.

"Are you authorized to stop it?"

"Let me put it this way. The creepy monitor guy gets on my nerves, and there is no way anyone on this planet could find the perp from the footage. I am best used here with you."

A. A. Dober

THIRTEEN

From the first time Juan had read about pigeon Sputnik traps, he'd been fascinated with their simplicity and their clever design. The trap was just a shelf attached to the middle of a box, really, that was built of sticks and walls made of chicken wire. The birds landed on the jutting shelf that resembled the landing pads of flying cars in *The Jetsons*. Then there were open bays set at a forty-five-degree angle that the birds could hop through, which put them on a level about eight inches lower, where there was food. Though the pigeons could hop in, they couldn't fly back out, because the openings only allowed them to squeeze through with their wings closed. If they wanted to fly out, there was simply no room. The trap was a one-way door, basically, into their home where the food awaited. The trap was then attached to the main aviary building, and the birds moved in to meet their partners or feed their young. It was a beautifully simple device that allowed them to enter at any time, leaving the pigeon keeper carefree about their arrival time.

But carefree was the opposite of what Juan was right now. He needed to figure out a rudimentary alarm

system. He needed to know the exact arrival time of
that last pigeon.

"Juan!" Virginia called.

"Qué" (What), he responded.

*"Tengo que salir. No puedo viajar sin mi estuche
de coser."* (I need to go out. I can't travel without my
sewing kit.)

"OK. ¡Aqui te espero, pero no te tardes porfa!"
(OK, I'll wait here, but don't be long, please!) he
screamed at the sky as he lay on top of a small parapet
wall about eight inches high as the entire roof was still
wet. He looked as if he could fall off with one hand
dangling off the edge. But the fall wouldn't be lethal,
because the house was only about ten feet high in its
entirety.

Then it dawned on him. Sewing thread! He quickly
concocted a simple alarm, a single strand of sewing
string traversing all three doors of the Sputnik trap,
attached to a small bell his mother kept in the dining
area. She rarely had help, but when she did, she loved
to call the cook with the tiny bell. Virginia kept all
sorts of traditions of a better time.

He found thread in the sewing machine; not all of it
was kept in the sewing kit Virginia went out for. He
quickly assembled the string system, allowing him to
leave the roof and continue his plans. He returned
below to pack all the household items, carefully placed
his mother's Dalí prints in a box and enclosed all six
prints in plastic bubble material, making sure they
were safe.
From time to time he carefully ensured that the
pigeons were fully burned to ash. He kept adding
lighter fluid to the steel drum and relighting it so that
the smoldering would continue.

FOURTEEN

It flapped around in circles at first, looking disoriented, but then it hooked south on the side of the building and flew directly across Mission Valley and the Interstate 8. The thirty-fifth pigeon was carrying a tiny GPS with enough battery power to send its location to cell towers around the globe for the next twenty-four to forty-eight hours. Cliff had to travel west to Morena Boulevard to cross the freeway and immediately was twenty minutes behind the bird. The chopper, on the other hand, followed a half mile behind with perfect accuracy.

"Cliff, you better get to 5 South," Brent said on the radio.
"Copy that," Cliff replied.

The team followed the blue dot. Brent kept calling ahead, anticipating the next location. He radioed National City and spoke to its police department, only to cancel any aid as the bird flew right over National City and into Chula Vista. Brent called Chula Vista, again to no avail. His last call was to San Ysidro, bordering Tijuana, and now the bird was in Mexico, as expected. All this in a ten- to fifteen-minute time span! Cliff was a good thirty minutes behind.

"Cliff, just keep going south," Brent said. "I will alert the police at the crossing. You will be escorted by a local police vehicle from that point on."

"OK. I will make contact at the border crossing," Cliff said.

The chopper was trailing the bird by only a few minutes. If the bird stopped, they would be in the immediate vicinity of the thief's lair, and the last thing Brent wanted was to alert him to the police presence. On top of that, the air traffic controller of the Tijuana International Airport was staying in contact with them to ensure that they did not conflict with any flight plan.

"Captain?" The chopper pilot spoke on the radio.
"Yes?" Brent asked.
"It's the airport tower. We are being told to stay put or detour around the area from here to the coast at three thousand feet. We cannot keep moving in a straight line."

Brent felt the nauseating halting motion of the helicopter, which felt like an amusement park ride. Dick looked white as a sheet and ready to vomit.

"Do as you are told; go around the airspace; we still can see the dot moving south," Brent ordered as he looked at the iPad and then clumsily grabbed it to get a closer look. Not being too savvy with technology, his mere touch sent the iPad to a different window and the dot was lost. Dick took the device back and immediately restored its function.

"Try not to touch the screen; hold it like this." Dick showed Brent.

The helicopter flew toward the sea and around the airport runway corridors. The Mexican police were aware of the presence of the helicopter and condoned the operation, but the team was expected to respect the integrity and safety of the airspace.

Then it happened.

A. A. Dober

FIFTEEN

The tiny bell rang once. Only once, and quite lightly. Juan heard it, left everything, and ran upstairs. There she was. Juan recognized her. She had given birth not long ago and was a special bird. Why she hadn't left the jewelry shop he didn't know. Maybe the birth had made her less attentive. In any event, she was here now. Home.

He took her and saw the leather strap bulging with the geometrical shaped object in it. With not a second to be lost, he quickly wrung her neck. He opened the satchel and saw the GPS blinking. Then he looked up at the sky and listened closely. All he could hear was the defending noise of the city all around him. Cars everywhere, honking, and noise, just immense and unceasing city noise. He ran down the stairs and into the backyard, jumping over his fence like a crazy person. If Virginia had seen him, she would have thought the devil himself was chasing her boy. He ran down between two homes, then onto the next street. About a hundred yards down, he hooked left into what seemed like a ravine. On this strange path, there was a concrete footbridge that connected the sides of the ravine. And at the bottom of the ravine was a two-way

road with a constant flow of traffic. Juan stopped in the
center of the footpath and looked below. The chain-
link fence meant to keep people safe was all that
separated him from a fall to certain death below.
People crossed back and forth here all day long,
passing and greeting one another politely. Juan waited,
holding the dead pigeon in his hand until the busiest
time arrived. A huge truck carrying gravel in an open
container approached. He put the bird through the links
with his hands and squeezed his left hand through the
chain link fence, holding the bird on the other side, and
then he quickly put his right hand through another hole
in the fence, grabbed the bird, and waited for the exact
moment when he saw the gravel below. He was about
to let go, then he stopped. He quickly opened the
leather sack and pulled the GPS from it. He dropped
only the GPS device.

The two seconds it took were enough for the GPS to
miss the cargo bay of the cement truck. Luckily, the
truck was carrying a double load, and a second
container followed the first, which was where the GPS
device landed. For an instant, Juan thought it would
land on the street—it barely made it into the second
container! The operation was a success, and Juan was
so happy. He brought the dead pigeon and his hands
back inside the fence and hid the bird in his clothing.
People kept crossing the bridge in their daily routine
and barely glanced at Juan. He sat there, waiting to see
what followed. About five minutes later, a speck
appeared in the sky in the distance. Slowly, it grew
until he could see it was a helicopter. He watched as it
moved diagonally toward the road. It was following
the truck into the freeway system of Mexico, and from
there, who knew how far. His heart raced and he
breathed long and hard to control his emotions, then he
sat up to finish his pigeon obliteration campaign. He
walked back into the property from behind his

mother's home and placed the thirty-fifth pigeon into the still-smoking steel drum, then added fuel that quickly shot flames into the air. Then he went up on the roof, whereupon he demolished the pigeon aviary. He pushed it off the roof and it fell undramatically and quietly onto the dirt floor. Juan burned all the wood components and neatly rolled up the chicken wire. He wanted all evidence down to the last feather incinerated beyond recognition, so he placed the rolled-up chicken wire into the fire and watched as the small feathers burned off the steel.

He was feeling a bit safer now about leaving for Mexico City. Getting there was more important than ever. He needed to leave the home that same afternoon but did not want to drive in the middle of the night. He would drive to Mexicali that evening and sleep in a motel there. From this day on, he knew he was going to play a new game and that he would be smart about it. He walked to his chained pit bull and gently petted him while removing the collar that was attached to the chain. He warmly embraced the dog as it eyed the street and the freedom it craved too much.
Go, be free. I won't keep you here against your will any longer, Juan thought.

The dog ran away like any wild animal would when released from a cage. It would probably be a statistic soon, faced with the harsh reality of Tijuana street life. Juan removed the leather collar from the chain and dropped it into the fire. By now, the chicken wire was all black and had no sign of feathers. He pulled it out and stomped on it, flattening it. He then dragged it out back and dropped it into the ravine that many residents used to dump the stuff they no longer valued. The bottom of the ravine was so filled with junk that nobody went there. It was a no-man's-land of wasted construction materials, rusted mattress springs, and debris. A truly toxic bottom to a ravine that, had it not been impacted by the presence of humans, would probably have been a beautiful, nature-filled ecosystem.

SIXTEEN

In the helicopter, Brent followed the moving truck until they reached the point where he needed to decide whether they should fly back to the United States or keep going—they were down to a half tank of gas. The bird would need to be flying over the highway system to follow the path they were on, but Dick didn't realize this was happening because the image on the iPad screen was zoomed in tight.

"We are at fifty percent right now, sir. We need to turn back unless we want to land in Mexico. Are we near the target?" The helicopter pilot asked.

"I don't care if we have to land in Mexico. We will follow the bird until we get to its destination," Brent said.

"OK, no need to raise your voice. I just needed to let you know that if we continue we will need to find a suitable landing spot to gas up so that we can return. That is all."

"Understood."

They followed the highway system and Dick began to sense the GPS becoming faint.

"Sir." Dick started.

"What now?" Brent asked.

"The signal is fading, see."

"I see the dot."

"It is flashing slower every time."

"Let's go closer."

"OK."

"Captain, please go faster. We need to get closer to the bird."

The helicopter accelerated forward and soon closed the gap between the red arrow and the blue dot. They followed and followed at the speed of the truck for what felt like an eternity. The gas gauge was on everyone's mind now. Helicopters can't glide and gas is an essential element to their safety. So every minute that the search continued, their fear of the chopper's eventual landing increased.

"It stopped. It stopped!" Dick shouted.

"Where?" Brent

"Here." He showed Brent a small grouping of buildings next to a freeway."

"Show him again," Brent ordered Dick to show the pilot for the tenth time the location of the blue dot.

"Captain, where are you going to land?"

"I see a truck stop ahead and lots of power lines. It won't be easy, but I will look around."

The chopper flew around the truck stop to where the gravel truck had parked with the GPS as part of its cargo. The truck driver went into the bathroom and saw the chopper making a roundabout over the truck stop area. Clearly he could read the English word for *police*, which is not all that different from "policía." He ignored it and proceeded about his business. Behind the truck stop, there was an empty parking lot, which was ideal for the helicopter to land. The Pemex gas station was also the ideal refueling station for the helicopter, and the pilot was happy to land there.

"Sir, I will refuel as fast as possible," the pilot said.

"We do not know if the bird will retake flight. Stand by until I give the order," Brent said.

"Yes, sir." The pilot looked at the copilot and mouthed the word *asshole*.

"Dick, let's go," Brent instructed Dick.

"OK."

They descended from the helicopter and made a beeline for the small restaurant and truck stop. The blue dot was over the restaurant, with the red arrow at the parking lot. Dick zoomed out to see more definition and at that instant, the blue dot began to blink. Dick's face turned white.

"What is it?" Brent asked.

"I hope it is not the end of the transmission. It seems as if the battery is dying," Dick said.

"No."

"Yes."

The truck backed out and began to move toward its southerly destination again. The blue dot reappeared but farther south on the road. Just as the truck moved. Then it happened—the dot disappeared from the screen.

"What happened?" Brent asked in a panic.

"It's gone," Dick said looking up at the sky.

"Do you see it?" Brent said.

"Not on my screen."

"I thought the batteries were supposed to last twenty-four hours. It's barely an hour."

"Well, we did use the GPS given to us. Who knows how full its batteries were. These things are not guaranteed."

The blue dot appeared again over the highway and farther south.

"Did you see?" Dick said.
"Yes, it is getting away," Brent said.
"No. It's not the batteries; it's the lack of cell towers in Mexico."
"So it is working, but only when it gets within range of a cell tower."
"Exactly."
"Back to the chopper."

They both ran toward the chopper, and the pilot was dismayed. He'd hoped to be able to get gas, fill the tank, and fly back to the States.

"Damn it. Here they come," he muttered to the copilot covering the microphone.
"Yep."

The chopper flew south, its occupants hoping to receive a new blue ping farther down the highway. It was increasingly clear to all that the likelihood of catching the bird was becoming less and less.

"What if the bird moves into an area with no cell towers?" Dick asked.
"Don't start trying to complicate matters. Stay positive," Brent said.

Cliff was at least thirty minutes away, driving toward the truck stop. His Chrysler seemed to have a magnet for potholes, and every single one he hit, he screamed "shit!" This case was beginning to be a pain in the ass, both figuratively and literally. His biggest fear was walking into a lair of Mexican thieves who were armed with better weapons than he was.

"Madonna! These roads are horrible!" Cliff complained.

"I know. Maybe you should slow down a bit," Ivory chirped.

"What, and get there too late?"

"It's not like we are anywhere near them. They are flying, remember. And they will ask for local backup. So yes, slow down!"

A. A. Dober

SEVENTEEN

Leaving Tijuana was a joy for Juan and Virginia, but
Juan did not want to leave any loose ends. He
explained to Virginia that it would be foolish to pay
rent during their trip to Mexico City, and that he could
return any time they needed. After all their
arrangement was month to month. He loaded the car
with the few possessions they owned and drove to the
first house in the low-income housing project. From
this home, one could see every car that entered or
exited the community, and owning the home was
essential if one wished to control the neighborhood.
The most powerful man in this project, *"El Buitre,"*
Juan's landlord, lived there. The vulture was like the
bird in his physical attributes, because he was a heavy
and big man. Yet the nickname came from his
profession and not his looks; he was considered a
vulture who preyed on the defenseless and the weak.
He was a jolly, happy, and funny man, but ruthless,
nonetheless. If you did not pay your rent, all his
amiable attitude disappeared and the face of a quasi-
sociopathic ruffian appeared in its place. Crossing a
person like Buitre was not recommended, and Juan
needed to end the relationship on good terms.

"Perame aquí" (Wait here), Juan told Virginia as she sat in the car.

Juan entered the house and found Buitre at his usual desk.

"Hola, Buitre," Juan said.
"Hola, Juan. ¿Ya está?" (Hi, Juan. Is it all done?) Buitre asked.
"Sí, te la deje mejor que cómo me la diste. Ya sabes a mi ma le gustaba limpia y bonita." (Yes, I left it better than how you gave it to me. You know my mom kept it spic-and-span.)
"Bien. ¿I mi lana?" (Good. And my cash?)
"Aquí está." (Here.)
"¿Y los pinches pichónes?" (And the damned doves?)
"Ya no se fueron." (They left.)

Juan handed six hundred-dollar bills to Buitre. The landlord counted the bills, was satisfied, and looked up.

"¿A dónde vas?" (Where are you going?) Buitre asked.
"No sé. A dónde me de el viento" (Don't know, wherever the wind takes me), Juan answered.

Buitre looked at him strangely but kept quiet. Juan had given his answer with such seriousness that it left no room for more questions. A huge man came in through the kitchen door. It was Buitre's righthand man, Pingüino, and he had heard the conversation.

"¿Juanito, te nos vas?" (Juanito, you are leaving us?) Pingüino asked.
"Hola, Pingüino, no te mire. Sí, voy pal sur unos meses. Cuando vuelva paso a verlos." (Hi, Penguin, I

didn't see you. Yes, I'm going south for a few months.
When I'm back, I'll look for you guys.)

"*Andale pues!*" (OK!) Penguin said.

"*Me voy porque mi ma me espera en el carro.*"
(I'm out of here; my mom is waiting in the car.)

"*Adiós, Juan.*"

Buitre just sat there emotionless and immediately
turned to Penguin.

"*Vete a la casa de Juan y revisala bien. Avisame
si esta lista.*" (Go to Juan's house and check it out. Let
me know if it is ready to rent.)

Juan drove off in the direction of Mexicali.

"*¿Lista?*" (Ready?) Juan asked his mom.

"*Lista.*" (Ready.) Virginia smiled.

There were two more hours of light, and getting to
Mexicali would take them about an hour and a half.
Juan had scouted a motel near the highway that led to
Sonora; tomorrow they would drive to Guadalajara and
then Mexico City. He had always wanted to see the
murals at the famous building by Orozco in
Guadalajara, and this would be his chance.

He would not travel south in the Camry. It had US
plates, and he needed the two thousand dollars that he
could get for it. Also, if anybody were looking for him,
tracking the car would be the easiest way to find him.
Mexicali was the last city where selling a US car in
Mexican soil was possible—you needed a permit to
drive a US car past there and into southern Mexico.

"*Pasado mañana vamos al Hospicio Cabañas,
Ma.*" (The day after tomorrow we will go to the
Hospicio Cabañas, Mom.)

"Qué padre, mi hijo." (Great, my son.)

She was not sad to leave Tijuana. Juan was acting like a grown man and very sure of their trip to Mexico City, which gave her a sense of security. Something good had happened to her son, and she attributed it to his reading the details of the lawsuit. Maybe he had matured fast, now that he knew what had really happened to his dad. They would spend the next two days arranging the freight of their belongings to Virginia's sister Esmeralda's home in Mexico City, good sleeping conditions in Guadalajara and finding good tickets for bus transportation.

"Lo único que sé, es que los Dalís y mis cosas personales se quedan con nosotros todo el tiempo. ¿Entiendes?" (The only thing that I know is that the Dalís and my personal belongings stay with us all the time. Understood?) Virginia was adamant.
"Claro que sí, Mamá." (Of course, Mom.)

EIGHTEEN

"We need gas. It is no longer safe," the helicopter pilot said.

"Do what you need," Brent said.

The pilot searched and found a small airport close to Ensenada on the Pacific coast of Mexico. The gravel truck had traveled south to this port city, where small hotels sprang up in mini-construction booms and busts. The fishing village was popular with tourists who found it close to Tijuana and did not feel like driving all the way south to Cabo San Lucas. The blue dot was pinging, moving south along the coast. The now close to two-hour flight was rapidly becoming a disaster in Brent's eyes.

The helicopter deviated to the airstrip and landed. The pilot arranged to get gasoline in a straightforward and quick manner. Local police met them there and provided support. Dick and Brent stayed in the helicopter, looking at the blue dot move on the screen. It was still moving west, but then it stopped on the other side of the peninsula that composes one side of Ensenada Bay.

"We have them!" Brent screamed.

"Calm down," Dick said. "The bird stopped before but then took off again. Let's wait and see."

"Stop being negative."

The blue dot was static. Brent was anxious, and he pushed the pilot to speed up his gas purchase. He approached the local law enforcement detail that had been called in and showed them the GPS with the blue dot.

"What is there?" Brent asked the Mexican cop.

"That is a, how do you say this, a job site, construction," the cop said.

"Exactly, an abandoned job site, perfect."

"No."

"What?"

"Not abandoned. That is exactly where they are building a new hotel."

"OK. Let's go there, but no sirens, proceed with caution."

The truck had arrived at the site and dumped its load of gravel, which would be used to mix with cement and sand in the making of the concrete needed for the foundation of the construction. The GPS, having been on top of the gravel, was now buried in about three feet of the stuff. The signal was still working, and the blue dot led the team of officers directly to the mountain of gravel. Dick stood over the pile and pointed down. The police enlisted three or four construction workers to dig for the GPS using shovels. Dick kept indicating the position as the iPad dictated.

In the meantime, Brent figured out that the material had just been delivered by a truck that had arrived from Tijuana and drew the logical conclusion. Dick ran with the GPS in his hand to Brent as he stood, defeated, by the rubble.

    "Got it." Dick had a huge smile when saying this.
    "And you are smiling, because?" Brent said.
    "I…"
    "Stop smirking; this is the end of the line. We go
back immediately, empty-handed, you fool."
    "I'm sorry, I was just happy the GPS worked."
    "It obviously didn't. It fell off the bird, you idiot."

Dick shut up. He had missed the bigger picture and
had been caught up in the tech aspect of the mission.
Then he realized that he was happy that it hadn't
worked. A confrontation with Mexican jewel thieves
was not what he wanted! They both assumed the GPS
fell off the bird and onto a moving truck. When this
happened was anyone's guess. It was the end of the
line. Brent walked with his head down and got back
into the refueled helicopter.

    "Let's go. That's it for this mission!" Brent
shouted.
    "Yes, sir!" the pilot fired back.
    "Cliff. Abort mission, it was a dead end." Brent
spoke into the receiver.
    "Copy that," Ivory chirped.
    "Is that you, Ivory? What are you doing here?"
Brent asked.
    "I am Cliff's partner, sir."
    "I know, but I had you checking the video."
    "That was a dead end as well, sir."
    "See you back at the office. Over and out."

The helicopter took off and left six Mexican patrol cars
at the construction site of a small hotel on the Pacific
Ocean. As they ascended, a single gray pigeon flew in
front of them, so close that they all saw it clearly.
Brent and Dick looked at each other. Then another

pigeon followed the first one, and the spell broke. They returned to the States empty-handed as the sun was setting, creating a spectacular pink clouded sky that made the disastrous end a bit less ugly.

NINETEEN

Guadalajara was a large city, the third most populated by Mexicans after Mexico City and Los Angeles. Its population was composed of all different levels of society like any large metropolitan city but with one small difference—there was less anonymity than in a city the size of New York or Mexico City. Guadalajara only had about a million and a half people compared to metropolitan cities in the tens of millions. In a way, it was not a fully mature metropolis and this made it less than ideal for fencing a diamond. Juan had to resist the urge to look for a jewelry store that bought diamonds. He knew that Guadalajara had more connections to San Diego than Mexico City, and that word could reach the authorities. He needed to lie low and make his first sale count. Mexico City had dealers with deep pockets and was far from the city where the crime had taken place. He would wait, even if he were afraid of running low on cash. The Camry only brought in fifteen hundred, because a spot sale always yielded less cash, but he was determined not to use his US credit cards again. He even cut them in half to make sure there was no way they could be used. Any credit sale would be traceable, and he had seen enough

movies about fugitives to know this. The bus to
Guadalajara and the taxi to the motel exhausted
Virginia, and he allowed her to sleep in. In the
afternoon, Juan took his mom to the famous murals.
He realized how much cheaper Mexico was when they
drove for a good fifteen minutes and the cab fare
totaled only five dollars. They walked into the huge
old building.

"Wow!" Virginia said.
"*Sí.* Wow," Juan agreed.

They stood, looking up at ceiling of the *Hospicio
Cabañas* where the famous muralist José Clemente
Orozco had painted his expressionistic scenes of fiery
figures flying in the sky. This was Mexico's equivalent
of the Sistine Chapel, and Orozco, the most painterly
and loose of the three famous muralists, had done as he
desired here. Rivera and Siqueiros had also painted
important murals, but Orozco was Juan's favorite, just
as the painter had been his father's favorite. The effect
was mesmerizing and unique. Virginia had taught Juan
about art once she started to take a serious look at art
in a desire to decorate her first home. Juan's father also
loved art, and for a time, the three shared this passion.
The Dalí prints his mom so deeply loved were the only
surviving element of a small collection the Merlos had
accumulated.

The bigger problem now would be to figure out how to
fence the diamonds and not squander the assets. Juan
was determined to have this nest egg last. Not having
been caught for the robbery did not guarantee that he
wasn't at risk when fencing the stones. On top of that,
there was the possibility of having someone steal his
loot, of having a fence rat on him, and of having the
cash sitting at home. All these problems had solutions,
and so Juan prepared a list of rules. If he kept to the

rules, he would be fine. "Not fencing a stone in a small town" was one of the first rules he had commited to memory, and he did not consider Guadalajara a big enough town.

Juan had studied carefully the mistakes made by criminals. It was not the crime but the mismanagement of the fruits of the crime that brought most criminals down. Even the criminal masterminds of the Great Train Robbery were now known. Not being caught was the first step, but the second was managing a lifetime of deception. Keeping Virginia in the dark would be the most difficult challenge. She would probably sense something was amiss but he would work at making sure she never knew it was illegal. A mother always believes her offspring are capable of great things and Juan would keep it that way. He was sure that she would keep loving him and that she trusted he was on the right path. He knew she had hated living on the border, and moving to Mexico City, even if in dire straits, seemed like a part of the solution.

He devised and memorized six rules for cleaning the assets:
Rule #1 Only fence one diamond at a time, and if possible, have it set in an old setting so the buyer believes he is buying an heirloom.
Rule #2 Always accept cash and only cash.
Rule #3 Always do so in disguise and use false names.
Rule #4 Only fence in large metropolitan cities, and always different ones, every time.
Rule #5 Never under any circumstances leave an electronic record of the money received.
Rule #6 Do nothing in haste, even if this means not buying a new home for a while and living modestly.

Juan knew this was going to be tough and he mulled in

his head all the future scenarios. His rules would be the only safe way. They required travel, but he would have the means. But the issue of the cash was a thorn— traveling with a lot of it was dangerous, and any amount over ten thousand dollars was a red flag to the authorities. So he devised a scheme to convert the assets into tangible property for the trip back after fencing a stone. This idea of transformed assets began to bounce around in his head and a new plan began to emerge. He would begin his transformation as soon as tomorrow, when they would reach Mexico City.

TWENTY

"That wraps up this case," Cliff said.

"I wish we could continue to hunt for this criminal," Ivory said.

"With what? We have no trace of where he went. At this point, we have very little we can do. Red flags in the diamond industry are the next step. If the criminal tries to unload the merchandise, we should get alerts. But that is for another division, and we need to move on. Don't worry, Ivory, he will mess up and he will be caught, it just won't be us doing the catching, and it won't be soon," Cliff said.

"I can't believe he got away with it."

"It is never just one person; I am sure he had accomplices."

"What if it was just one guy?"

"Then it will be much, much harder to get him."

Cliff and Ivory had just stood up from their cubicles, where they were finishing up with all the red tape, when Brent saw Leo. Brent was in his glass-enclosed supervisor's office, but he immediately walked over to Cliff and Ivory.

"Fuck me," Brent uttered.

"What's up, boss?" Cliff asked.

"It's Leo Stephens. The insurance investigator, former cop, and former partner," Brent said.

Brent sat down next to his assistants, away from his office and in essence hiding out until Leo found him.

"And you hate him because…?" Ivory asked.

"He just thinks he knows it all," Brent said.

"We need to help him on the flying diamonds?" Ivory asked again.

"Yep. He's the go-to guy for the insurance companies. What a hassle," Brent said.

"Why?" Ivory asked again, now getting looks from Cliff and Brent.

"Whenever there is an unsolved case, the insurance companies have to pay up. So Leo, he tries to show us what we did wrong," Brent said.

"And this guy is difficult?" Cliff asked.

"To say the least," Brent said.

Leo Stephens walked down the corridor, dressed in an impeccable black suit with a matching thin black tie and a super-clean pressed white shirt. He looked more like a Secret Service agent than an insurance investigator, and a very well-tailored agent at that. His shoes were black leather, Bostonian style and Italian made. His tie, if one looked closely enough, was embossed with a stylized jaguar silhouette, followed by an identical but upside-down jaguar silhouette, in shiny black and shinier black. It was a Hermès tie worth over one hundred dollars. The suit was handmade to his exact size. He walked with his chin up and with purpose, looking as cocky as a human possibly can. He was a six-foot-three-inch, forty-year-old white male with shiny black hair and deep blue eyes. Ivory looked up and her mouth opened slightly. She felt like she was watching the pages of a magazine in three dimensions.

"Brent! There you are," Leo said.

"Oh. Hi, Leo," Brent said.

"I need everything on the Quayles Jewels case," Leo ordered.

"It's not ready," Brent said.

"But we just…" Ivory trailed off, noticing that Brent was glaring furiously at her.

"Maybe we will have it by the end of the day," Cliff said, saving Ivory.

"I hope you are not stalling me, Brent. I need to get this guy fast," Leo said.

"That is very ambitious, considering…" Ivory paused.

"Considering? And who, pray tell, is this beautiful lady?" Leo said, half-mocking, half-serious.

"Detective Ivory Godwit." Ivory stood up.

"Well, Ms. Godwit, I do need a copy of all the files you have on this perp. Everything," Leo said, looking her in the eye.

"Ivory, Leo here was my partner back in the day. But he went private," Brent said.

"Really, why?" Ivory asked.

"The short answer? Money," Leo replied.

"And the long answer?" Ivory asked.

"I enjoy catching my prey. I have more resources, and the insurance companies never forget," Leo said.

"I'll have your file later today, Leo," Brent reiterated.

"How about lunch?" Leo said to Ivory, ignoring Brent.

"I'm afraid I can't. I am still writing my report on the flying diamonds," Ivory said.

"The flying diamonds, huh. That is what you are calling it?" Leo asked.

"That is what happened," Ivory said, blushing a little from his attention.

Brent and Cliff looked at each other and sat down
again. Evidently Ivory had charmed Leo, and the small
interaction became a courting.

"I wish you would grant me some of your time? I
would love to hear your version of events, and I also
think I would enjoy your company," Leo added.
"Is that an invite?" Ivory clumsily responded.
"Maybe. How about dinner tonight? That is an
invite," Leo said.

Ivory had planned to see Cliff that evening after work
for their usual fish and chips at Wahoo's in Point
Loma. She promptly blew Cliff off. "I would like
that," she said.

Leo grabbed one of Ivory's cards from her desk.

"I'll call you," he told her.
"Five o'clock!" Leo reminded Brent.

He left as elegantly as he had arrived.

"Oh! I do hate him," Brent said softly.
"He's dreamy," Ivory countered softly.
"I thought we were going to Wahoo's," Cliff said
loudly.
"Count me out tonight," Ivory said.
"If he calls you," Cliff said.
"Oh, he will. I know it," Ivory said.
"Ivory, grab the file and copy everything in it,"
Brent ordered her.
"Yes, sir." Ivory picked up the file with about one
hundred pages and went off to the copy room.

TWENTY-ONE

The first step entailed finding a secure location for the diamonds. Juan's mom's sister introduced him to her Banamex bank manager, who helped Juan open a new checking account. In the Mexican naming system, people used a first name, and a second name when they had one, followed by a paternal last name and a maternal last name. Juan Luis Merlo Rodriguez did not match the name on Juan's US driver's license, which was Juan Merlo Rodriguez. The US system continually made various accounts of Juan as Juan M. Rodriguez, and this made him furious, but not now. His Banamex account was under the name Juan Luis Merlo, and it didn't match his US driver's license or US passport. Without anyone knowing, he went back to the bank and rented a safe-deposit box, then returned again that afternoon with a zipped plastic bag full of diamonds. That evening, his head felt heavy, and a deep sense of peace and well-being enveloped him, giving him that night his best, most restful sleep in weeks. He slept on the couch of his aunt's home; his mom was in a spare bedroom left empty by his college-age cousin. His mom was not happy about staying there more than three evenings, and Juan felt pressured by her concern.

"Ya sabes que los muertos y los invitados apestan a los tres días" (You know that corpses and guests stink in three days), Virginia kept saying.

So Juan spent every minute of his time doing what needed to be done. He soon found a decent apartment in the swanky and cosmopolitan neighborhood of Polanco. By Mexico City standards, it was fantastic, and it cost about one thousand five hundred dollars a month. But the owner demanded two months' rent as a security deposit. So Juan needed more money than he had available in cash. His mom had to stay put with her sister while he saw about renting a place for them. Virginia was worried that Juan might not be able to support them and feared for the future. But Juan's confidence eventually rubbed off on her, and she believed in him as never before.

Juan rented a motel room near his aunt's house and entered carrying one of his suitcases, which contained all the things he needed to disguise his appearance. He exited the motel room dressed in a black suit, black shirt, and black tie, his hair curled like a dancer's in a movie. He wore large sunglasses and moved with an effeminate walk. He did this even while he waited for a public bus, knowing he annoyed the gay haters, who in Mexico City were notoriously more loudspoken and violent from those in San Diego. He rode the bus south to the famous Mexico City flea market with a presence worthy of a surreal painting. He walked strangely along stalls decorated in old tapestries next to Japanese Manga cartoon stands and followed by one after another tiny plot of old trinkets and used possessions. The market was called La Lagunilla, which means *the small lagoon*. Juan was amused that the flea market had a name that required the article to sound like a repetition of the name itself. If one just said *"lagunilla,"* people would not be sure of the reference.

But as soon as one qualified it as La Lagunilla, they immediately recognized it. Of course, having been founded in the 1560s helped the market's fame as a place for buying and selling goods. Now, 456 years later, the market had a reputation for being the place to go when one is looking for all sorts of antiques, art, electronics, and other valuables. Adding to its prestige was the fact that you could always find recently stolen articles there. For decades, families in Mexico City had repurchased recently burglarized family heirlooms there.

Juan left a wake of comments behind him as he moved around. If anybody remembered anything, it was not that a man bought a ring setting, but rather that a strange, effeminate man drew comments and laughter behind his back. Juan looked for a ring with a fake two-carat diamond. He needed the setting to look old and to be real gold or platinum, not false. An heirloom of a real diamond is never set in a fake setting, and he was determined to look hard for one. The job proved simple enough, however, and for one thousand five hundred pesos or a little under a hundred dollars, he bought a corny setting for a two-carat diamond holding a cubic zirconia. He called a street cab and jumped into the back of a small VW bug with no passenger front seat. On the way to the motel, he reminded himself of Rule #3—*Never return to your safe place in disguise.*

Juan stopped the cab a few blocks before reaching his motel and entered a Vips coffee shop dressed like an effeminate and stylized man, proceeded to the bathroom, and, in a stall, transformed to a regular guy. It was not hard. He took off the large sunglasses, jacket, tie, and black shirt and put them into a folded black bag he had carried with him. Underneath, he wore a clean white T-shirt that immediately changed his appearance. Then using the sink, he quickly rinsed his hair with water. Just like that, Juan was back. He dropped the effeminate movements and quickly left Vips, walking back to the motel, the ring hidden in his pocket.

Perhaps he had inherited his skills from his father, or maybe he had an old watchmaker ancestor he did not know about, but metallurgy came easy to him, in this case, bending without breaking the setting in order to substitute the real diamond. Using two sets of pliers held with both hands, he pried the upside-down ring gently until the zirconia fell out. Then he reversed the maneuver. To accomplish this, he used a little roll of two-sided tape on a Q-tip that he held between his teeth. Essentially, he needed three hands, and the Q-tip in his lips became the third hand. The tape held the diamond gently, and he inserted it where the zirconia had been. As soon as he released the pressure on the metal, the stone was trapped perfectly in the ring. Small gaps were easily adjusted with pressure on the soft gold. He planned to buy better equipment, but always generic stuff. The last thing he needed was to have professional jewelry equipment with him that might cause unnecessary questions or suspicion and could become circumstantial evidence.

The first fence is always the highest, Juan thought.

He needed support, and therefore he planned to enlist Virginia. She was not an accomplice, and Juan knew she didn't suspect anything. It was unimaginable that she even knew of the diamond heist, because she never read the newspaper and rarely watched the news. In Tijuana her concept of news was limited to local events and even more to local gossip. Also, because of the move, the TV was packed away, which meant she had no chance of seeing or hearing about the heist. Juan desperately needed the working capital to continue his liquidity plan, but he was not going to take chances. Virginia, therefore, was the ticket. He took the newly set ring back to his aunt's home, hoping to find his mom alone. His timing was just right—his Aunt Esmeralda had left for work, and Virginia was alone except for the maid. Esmeralda worked as secretary for an important chief executive who ran a private medical device company.

Juan rang the bell outside the modest home, which had a small grass garden used as a parking lot, with stones placed in rows to identify parking spaces. It was an old home in the San Miguel Chapultepec neighborhood of Mexico City, bordering the Roma neighborhood. Juan knew that Esmeralda actually disputed which of the two neighborhoods her house belonged in, since it had a San Miguel Chapultepec address but she had to explain to visitors that it was in the Roma neighborhood so that they could find it. Mexico City was arcane and complex, its signage even more so. In this city there were continual changes to street direction, street names, and numbers. Many homes display two numbers, the new one and another with "formerly" displayed beside it. It was almost as if the authorities were trying to create more confusion and more traffic, rather than alleviating it.

Juan waited for the aging maid to open the lock the chain holding together the steel doors. It was almost comical that the entire safety of the house depended on a chain that could be bolt-cut by any amateur thief. The maid moved as if in slow motion, mimicking most of what happened in Mexico City as compared to San Diego. Juan was almost ready to trample her in his haste.

"Ma. Ma," Juan called.
"*¿Qué pasa?*"

"¡No vas a creer lo que me encontre!" (You won't believe what I found!) Juan exclaimed.

"Espera, estoy viendo las noticias. Este robo paso en San Diego. Ve." (Wait, I am watching the news. This theft happened in San Diego. Look.)

Images of the flying pigeons leaving the Quayles Jewels building and passing in front of the camera were showing on the old Sony, which was almost identical to Virginia's but larger. Juan felt his blood rush. This he hadn't expected. The crime was notable due to the use of the birds, and it was making worldwide news. Now everybody in the world would hear of the flying diamond heist! Juan could only hope that the news cycle would have a very short life span and some shark attack or NASCAR crash would supplant it in viewers' memories. But the mind of a person who has just done something as bold as Juan can play tricks. Virginia could easily connect his pigeons to the pigeon theft, and this made him extra nervous.

Juan was caught in a mental trap; he craved recognition for having pulled off the crime, but he knew that it could be his downfall. He knew that the desire to achieve respect as the result of getting away with a crime was perhaps the number one reason most criminals were caught. Juan panicked and went to his room, abandoning the plan to ask Virginia to be his first fence.

"Estoy muerto, ma. Voy a descansar un poco en tu cuarto." (I'm beat, Mom. I am going to rest a bit in your room.)

"OK," Virginia said.

Lying in the small bedroom and smelling the recently watered ivy on the fence directly across from the open window, Juan was reminded of other times he had spent in Mexico City. It was a distinctive smell, mixed with the feeling of the home itself, made of cold bricks and mortar, a contrast with the sheetrock and stud houses of America. Juan wondered if such feelings were normal; did everybody sense such things? He was de-stressing from having his mom learn about the diamond heist in San Diego. He relaxed completely when an idea struck him. Keeping Virginia out of his plan was the best possible solution. If she ever asked him about the pigeon theft he would deny any involvement. Keeping Virginia ignorant was the best way of protecting her. Now he felt he had a solution in impersonating a typical middle-aged widow. Having played a heavyset white man and a gay Mexican dandy emboldened him to take this next step. He knew that being in Aunt Esmeralda's home was uncomfortable for his mom. Moving to Polanco would be perfect, because it would be a clear step up from Esmeralda's mediocre house and give his mom the added status she yearned for. He fell into a slumber and relaxed on the bed while smelling Mexico City.

Juan woke up to the abrupt noise of a car horn. Even the side streets weren't immune to noisy traffic. He went into his aunt's bedroom and rifled through her clothing, feeling once more like a thief. She was a little smaller than he was, but there must be something he could use. On the upper shelf in a box, he found some dresses that were from a time when she was heavier. It was just perfect, because they wouldn't be missed. This wasn't theft; he would return them later. Juan placed the dresses in his backpack without anyone noticing.

That evening the family sat for dinner in the small home that belonged to Roberto and Esmeralda Espinaza. Esmeralda was married to an aging history expert with a desire to retire and live off his pension. Professor Roberto Espinaza's life had been a constant commute and process of repetition that left him tired and broken. He was bitter, but quirky enough to throw in a stinging comment every now and then. Esmeralda was a working mother, and her three kids had now left home to start their own lives through marriage or work. Today two of her daughters would come to see their cousin and aunt, Juan and Virginia Merlo. Family reunions were not common for Juan and Virginia, but they welcomed the experience. The missing cousin was the male son, who had moved to Cancun in search of a better life. He was now assistant manager at the Kristal Hotel and doing well for himself.

"*¿Qué tal San Diego, Juan?*" (Tell us about San Diego, Juan?) Esmeralda asked.

"*Muy duro. La vida en los Estados Unidos no es lo que parece. Sin educación no te dan buenas chambas. Yo me la paso trabajando y apenas salimos adelante*" (Life is hard in the States. Without a college degree, you can't get a good job. I work all day, and we barely get by), Juan said.

"*Suenas amargado*" (You sound bitter), Cousin Mariel said.

"*Sí. Estoy, bueno estaba*" (Yes. I am, well, was), Juan replied.

"*¿Estabas? En el pasado. ¿Qué paso?*" (You were? In the past. What happened?) Mariel asked again.

"*¡Me siento en la inquisición! Pero te cuento. Finalmente tome las riendas de mi vida. Por eso la amargura se va a quedará atrás.*" (I feel as if I am in the Inquisition. But I'll tell you. Finally I took control of my life. That is why all the bitterness will be left behind.)

"*Ujule. Que bien, ¿y qué quiere decir eso?*" (Wow. Good, and what does that mean?) Mariel sarcastically asked.

"Primita, yo ya no voy a tratar de medio hacerla en los Estados Unidos. Voy a abrir un negocio aquí y hacerla en grande. Veras" (Little cousin, I am no longer going to try to make it in the United States. I am opening a business here and will make it big. You will see), Juan responded.

"¿Un negocio de que tipo?" (What kind of business?) Mariel's husband, Rodrigo, asked.

"Una tienda de antigüedades y consignación" (An antique and consignment shop), Juan calmly said.

"¿Desde cuando?" (Since when?) Virginia said.

"Lo he estado planeando desde hace mucho, Ma" (I've been planning it for a long time, Mom), Juan said, even though it was a very recent idea.

"No sabia" (I had no idea), Virginia said.

"¿Pero no necesitas capital y una clientela para hacer eso? Digo, acabas de llegar" (But don't you need capital and a clientele to do that? I mean, you just got here), Rodrigo asked.

"Pato. No molestes a Juanito" (Pato. Don't bother Juan), Mariel told her husband Rodrigo, using his nickname.

"No queria molestar" (I didn't mean to bother), Pato said.

"No es molestia. Yo se que es difícil pero tengo mis ahorros y los Dalís de mamá van a ayudar a jalar gente. No pienso venderlos sólo usarlos de gancho para comenzar" (It's no bother. I know it is hard, but I have some savings, and I plan to use my mom's Dalís to showcase the shop. I don't intend to sell them, just use them as magnets), Juan said.

"Parece que lo tienes bien planeado" (You seem to have it all figured out), Aunt Esmeralda said.

"Lo tengo" (I do), Juan said.

"Sabias que hay un nuevo museo de Carlos Slim" (You know there is a new museum donated by Carlos Slim?) Mariel said, changing the subject.

"Sí. Me encantaría ir" (Yes. I'd love to go), Juan said.

"¿Sí puedo te llevo la semana que entra, vale?" (If I can, I will take you next week, OK?)

"Hecho" (It's a fact), Juan responded.

"¿No por molestar, pero qué sabes de antigüedades y de arte?" (Not to be a pest, but what do you know of antiques and art?) Rodrigo pestered.

"Rodrigo, no se más ni menos que muchos, pero es un sentimiento realmente. Es cuestión de gustos. Ademas voy a estudiar la carrera de historia del arte en un instituto en Las Lomas" (Rodrigo, I don't claim to know more than others, but it is about feelings and taste. On top of that, I have plans to do the art history major at a school in Las Lomas), Juan said.

"Ya no hablemos de eso. ¿Oyeme, Juan, que paso con la novia que tenias? Mi tía decía que era muy bonita." (Let's change the subject. Hey, Juan, what about your girlfriend? My aunt said she was very beautiful). Mariel looked at Virginia when she said *aunt*.

"Sí, estaba guapa, pero las gringas no sirven para largo plazo" (Yes, she was pretty. But American girls do not work out in the long run), Juan said.

"Estaba preciosa" (She was gorgeous), Virginia interjected.

"¿Como esta eso?" (How's that?) Mariel asked.

"Para resumir. Los gringos ven a los mexicanos como una sola cosa. Básicamente jardineros" (To make a long story short, Americans see all Mexicans as gardeners), Juan said, and Pato laughed out loud.

Professor Espinaza, listening, made humming noises, a habit he had when he wanted to quiet the table. When they all looked at him, he said, *"Los Americanos son simples y no entienden que en México escuchabamos la ópera antes de que ellos mataran a los indios."* (Americans are simple and don't understand that in

Mexico we were listening to the opera before they crudely killed the Indians.)

They all looked at one another with the familiar here-we-go-again look. Professor Espinaza detected this and didn't say another word on that topic.

Dinner continued, and the conversation turned to many topics. Nobody talked about Juan's plans anymore. Virginia didn't recognize her son. He was so secure and strong in his opinions. She felt good about living in Mexico City.

Eventually the conversation flowed to politics, and they all agreed the new government was returning to the corrupt antics of the past. The general lack of safety of the city was again the main complaint of all of them. Professor Espinaza hummed again and everyone listened. He summarized the issue. *"La inseguridad es un problema mientras los criminales vayan impunes. Si el gobierno averiguara bien y encarcelara a los criminales no habría inseguridad. Punto."* (Social safety is a problem as long as there is impunity. If the government investigated crimes and jailed the criminals, there would be no problem. Period.)

Juan couldn't help but smile. Impunity is what he needed most at this point. He had no fear of the Mexican authorities—they had their hands full. The US authorities would be the ones to come calling, but only if he made a mistake. He needed to get rid of all the diamonds and shelter his money. Voicing his design of a business in the form of a consignment store made it a possibility. Having the backing of three to four million dollars after fencing the diamonds made it a reality.

TWENTY-TWO

Leo was a stickler for detail, and this included his attire. He was fastidious about color coordination and perfectly pressed suits. He also wore different ties almost all year round. His tie collection numbered in the hundreds, and this made him feel special. Some people are just happy with themselves, but Leo was never happy. His whole appearance emulated a happy, successful individual, and this could have been the case had he not measured himself against such high standards. He was never good enough, there was always a better route to take, a better path to achieve, a luckier individual than he, a better-dressed man. He sat all alone that evening in his office, poring over the police reports and the video images of the crime. It was perfect—the perfect crime.

He read the account about the GPS that was placed on the bird, and how they had flown a helicopter, tracking it all the way to San Felipe. It was a good report, but something about it was nudging his subconscious. He was a seasoned police investigator, and his instincts almost never failed him. Any discrepancy had to be investigated, and so far, nothing about the case was breaking his way. Except the GPS report. He picked up the phone and called the precinct.

"Captain Brent Argus, please," Leo said.

"He is not available. Whom may I say is calling?" Cliff said, recognizing Leo's distinct voice.

"Leo. Leo Stephens, working for TIPCO."

"Oh. Yes, Leo. I will let him know you called."

"Is this Cliff?"

"Yep."

"Cliff, it is you I am looking for."

"Really? How can I be of service?"

"Well, I am going over the account of tracking the bird into Mexico."

"Yes, and?"

"Well, I was wondering if I could get the raw data."

"I don't know what that is. Can you be more specific?" Cliff was breaking Leo's balls, because he hated that Ivory had taken a liking to him.

"I need the name and number of the IT guy who tracked it. Is that clear enough?"

"Crystal."

There was a pause during which Leo actually thought Cliff would help him.

"I don't have that information," Cliff lied.

"May I speak with someone who might have it?" Leo asked, now frustrated.

"Brent is out."

"You already told me that. My question is, may I speak to someone who knows who the IT guy is? Maybe your superior?"

"I am the most senior person at the station right now."

Leo hung up.

"Hello?" Cliff spoke into the click.

Cliff knew he'd gone too far, but he didn't care. It was better to ask for forgiveness than to help the SOB.

***

Meanwhile, Leo knew he would get the skinny in a few hours when he met Ivory for dinner at the Outback in Mission Valley. Their dinner date was set for 6:00 p.m., and he was more than ready and actually overdressed for San Diego. Anyone with a tie was clearly overdressed anywhere in San Diego and probably in all of California.

He arrived at the Outback and found Ivory waiting for him in the reception area, wearing a beautiful summer dress and looking great. The simple fact that she was not in pants and carrying a weapon and all the other gadgets made her light and cheery.

"You look amazing!" Leo said from the heart.
"Thanks." Ivory looked down shyly as she said this.

They sat in a two-person booth by the bar area, and both found that looking at the other was a pleasant experience. Ivory had the preconceived notion that someone as good-looking as Leo was a setup for disaster. As it happened he was more like a Clark Kent than a James Bond, and she found him to be likable. Leo was truly unaware of his good looks and did not know how to profit from them.

"We saw the birds flying out of the store and thought it was a curious thing. Like a fireworks show or a quick circus trick. It was so fast. But we had no idea they were carrying the loot!" Ivory said with much excitement.

"Do you know how one bird was trapped behind?" Leo asked.

"That was entirely Elliot Quayle's doing. He dragged himself over and pushed the door shut before the last bird flew out of his office."

"Do you think that was suspicious? I mean, it feels as if Elliot might have known what was going on?"

"Well, he did know. He saw the perp placing the diamonds on the birds one by one. So he knew they were leaving with his fortune. He tried to stop them but only succeeded in stopping one."

"Yes, yes, it makes sense. But let me tell you that in my line of work, insurance, the number one suspect is always the owner."

"Elliot? I don't think so. Why?"

"Well, they get paid twice, you see. If they steal their own jewels, they get paid for them in full. Plus, they still have the jewels. A very high percentage of these thefts are tied in with an owner. More so than the employees."

"Wow. That is interesting." Ivory looked in his eyes, bedazzled, although she knew all that he explained.

"Nah. It's boring, and I know it. Insurance conversations always are. Let me ask you one last question, and we can leave the theft behind."

"What is that?"

"Do you know the name of the IT guy who tracked the bird?"

"Dick. You mean Dick from the IT department. He went on the helicopter with Brent."

"Yes, do you know his full name?"

"Dick Greyson; he works at our office. A bit geeky but efficient."

Ivory said this as Leo wrote something on his telephone. He was already texting an e-mail to Dick—

using the precinct's employee format, first initial, period, last name, @ symbol, and pd.sandiego.gov— by the time she was finishing her statement.

"Thanks. Now to you. Where did you grow up?" Leo asked, sending the e-mail at the same time. The familiar flying sound of the iPhone was heard.

They spent the evening relaxed and having a good time. Ivory liked Leo, and his presence took her mind off all her other suitors. She could easily see herself fitting in his neat and precise world, but the question was more complicated in the reverse. Upon his bringing her home, the moment of truth arrived, and she was ready as she stood in front of her apartment complex in Tierra Santa.

"Well, I had a lovely night," Ivory said.
"So did I," Leo said and moved closer.

They both moved slowly toward each other and when their lips touched, it happened for Ivory. She felt a tingling sensation that rushed as if on a superhighway throughout her body. The kiss was wonderful, and Leo sensed that he had done something right. She grabbed his shoulders and pressed her body closer to his. Leo kissed her again and again. They moved into her place without another word and made love in her bedroom.

About an hour later Leo raised on one elbow and leaned over her.

"Don't take this the wrong way, but I need to get back to my place," he said.
"I didn't invite you to stay," Ivory said.
"I know. I am being presumptuous; it is just that I would love to stay. I just don't have the time. I am buried in reports to finish reading and need to find the flaw in the case."

"What if there is no flaw?"

"That is the first rule of law enforcement—the crime is always flawed. Always."

"I looked, you know. This crime is exceptional. We closed the case, because we have no leads. Nowhere. Zip. I mean, we even asked the bums on the streets, to see if they'd noticed something, but talk about unreliable witnesses!"

"I have a hunch, and that is why I need to go."

"What is it?"

"I got this e-mail from your IT guy with the information I asked for."

"Dick? He responded so soon?"

"You know geeks, they are always online. I need to pore over this data."

Leo went home, and as he got into his car, he felt a pang of emotion run through him. He couldn't resist and went back up the single flight of stairs and down the open corridor, back to door number 209. He knocked, and Ivory opened the door.

"What is it? Are you OK?" Ivory asked.

Her lips were met with a kiss. He kissed and kissed her. Then he turned around and left again. He didn't say a word. He left all communication to the kiss. Ivory was stunned. Was this really happening? She was so happy being left alone to ponder the significance of a kiss. And what a great kiss it had been!

Leo spent the evening looking at all the data from the GPS and finally found what he was looking for—two important discrepancies. First, the time of the trip from start to finish was too long. According to the data it took the pigeon over four hours to travel to San Felipe and these animals manage seventy miles an hour.

According to his calculations, the trip should have taken only half that time. The second was the path of the bird, which ignored all roads until it hit Tijuana, and particularly southern Tijuana. Then the path followed roads religiously. Of course nobody cared to look at the path itself, but only at the starting and stopping points. He found two flaws. Maybe the GPS fell onto a truck, but it was a starting point. He carefully noted the location where the GPS began to follow the road. That would be his destination tomorrow.

A. A. Dober

TWENTY-THREE

Sometimes a bold step into a new arena is unpleasant, sometimes it is the beginning of an addiction, and sometimes it is just a good thing. Dressing like a woman in perfect attire and makeup was weird but empowering to Juan. He didn't feel a sexual emotion in what he was doing, but he did feel a complete freedom. It was the ecstasy of anonymity. The difference in the men around him—their willingness to move out of his way and be polite—was strange, but it worked for him. He knew that once he was out of the disguise, that woman he had created in flesh and blood was no longer. Like the pigeons that had come and gone from the Quayles store, so did this short-lived female person disappear. It was all quite bizarre, but he pulled it off beautifully. It took him two hours in the motel room to become a strange but convincing woman. He knew he did not need to be attractive—that would be asking too much. But he needed to be just feminine enough so that there would be no doubt he was a woman. The greatest hurdle was age. He wanted to appear older, so that fencing the first diamond would be believable. Latex wrinkles were the solution, and he crafted some for wrinkles around the eyes, then some for the forehead, and finally, some for bags for under his eyes.

His voice was also not a difficult task. He had always been a high-toned kind of person, and many times on the phone he was confused with a female. All he needed to do was to think like a woman, and his voice was believable. He was becoming a master at makeup and role-playing, and he was ready to go and meet Mr. Becker.

The Joyeria Becker jewelry store was located in the Polanco District Juan aimed to live in. It was on a large street named after the first president of Czechoslovakia, Masaryk Boulevard. It sat opposite the Hermès store and next to Zegna, in the best boutique shopping district of the city.

Simon Becker had made a fortune in jewelry by copying the best stores in the world. His system was identical to a Tiffany or a Harry Winston, and he aimed to emulate them as often as possible. He sent his children to the best design schools in the world and had cornered the Mexican luxury market that was looking to save a little over the foreign competition. Of course Tiffany, Cartier, and Winston were more expensive, but Becker's quality was almost the same. The most aristocratic Mexican families favored Joyeria Becker, especially if they needed to be nationalistic, so most politicians' wives shopped there. In essence, Joyeria Becker was the "Mexican Tiffany's."

Juan left the motel in full female attire and carrying a large leather handbag. He walked for two blocks and looked for a restaurant he could use to alter his appearance again. He entered the restaurant and went to the restroom, where he put on a honey-colored trench coat. He left the restaurant and hailed a street cab to take him to Becker's. On the way there, he removed the gabardine once more, rolled it into a small ball and placed it back in his handbag. He didn't need this safety measure, but it was a precaution. If street cameras were recording, he would have entered the restaurant appearing one way, and exited looking another. On top of that many places had entrances on two streets and when he could use this he would try and use a different exit.

The cab drove in traffic for close to thirty minutes, even though it was only a few kilometers in distance. Juan had no choice but to remain in the cab; the shoes he wore would not allow him to walk that far. Entering Becker's as a lady required removing the gabardine so that the floral dress he wore displayed his features. Having a prosthetic bra and small hips made his body very feminine, and he walked quite so. The guard at the door immediately opened the jewelry shop door, and the delicious, cool air of the AC hit Juan on his makeup-encrusted face. He was happy to feel it. Inside, the shop looked like any other high-end jewelry store—very different compared to the huge size of Quayles. It was quaint and elegant, with beautiful, self-lit wood cases filled with dazzling jewels. The back of the shop had a spiral maple staircase that in and of itself was a jewel of carpentry. Juan walked straight to the only gentleman serving customers in the store, knowing that a woman would be much more likely to catch him in his game. The gentleman was Ricardo Becker, the son of the owner and a reluctant employee. Juan sensed that this junior employee would rather be playing with his friends on this sunny summer day.

"*¿Disculpe?*" (Excuse me?) Juan asked.

"*Sí, digame señorita*" (Yes, miss, how can I help you), Ricardo said.

"*Gracias por lo de señorita, joven pero necesito*

*hablar con el señor Becker sobre una pieza que
necesito vender."* (Thank you for calling me miss,
young man, but I need to see Mr. Becker about a piece
I am looking to sell.)

*"Mi padre no compra piezas así. De gente que
entra de la calle."* (My dad doesn't buy pieces like
that. From strangers off the street.)

"Ya lo sé. Pero esto es diferente." (I know, but
what I have is different.)

"¿De qué manera es diferente?" (In what way?)

"Eso lo veo con el." (I'll show him only.)

"Hmm," Ricardo said.

Ricardo walked backward a few steps, stopped, and
looked back at Juan in his disguise. Juan was happy it
was the owner's son and stared right back at him.
Ricardo had revealed to a stranger that he was a
Becker. Juan could see that Ricardo was a bit
disoriented and confused, not knowing that it was
because he had broken a tenet of the strict guidelines
of safety that his family's Mossad security company
had.

"Espere aquí" (Wait here), Ricardo ordered.

Juan stayed there, looking at the jewels in the case and
avoiding eye contact with any employees, particularly
females. The vibe he gave did not encourage anyone to
approach. Ricardo went up to the second floor and
entered his dad's office. He quickly explained that the
lady was clearly selling something, and perhaps it
could be profitable. His father stopped working on his
books and looked up at the wall of monitors in the
front of the office.

"¿Cuál es?" (Which one?) Simon Becker said.

"Esa." (That one.) Ricardo pointed at monitor
three.

"Mándamela" (Send her up), Simon said.

Juan was getting a bit nervous by the time he heard the son coming down. The nature of his nerves was not related to the transaction or to his having a diamond in his purse; he was more concerned with not being detected as a man. He followed Ricardo up the stairs and went into the elegant office of Simon Becker.

"Pásele, sientese por favor. ¿En que puedo servirle?" (Come in, sit down please. How can I be of service?) Simon said.

"Tengo que vender este anillo, pero es muy bueno y no quiero ni enseñarlo en lugares de empeño." (I need to sell this ring, but it is very good, and I don't want to even show it to pawn stores.) Juan took the ring from his pocket and gave it to Simon.

"Señora, yo no me dedico a comprar joyas a personas." (Madame, I don't buy jewels from individuals.) Simon held the ring in his hand.

"El problema es que son 3 y medio quilates" (The problem is that it's three-and-a-half carats), Juan said.

"El montaje no me interesa" (The mounting is not of my interest), Simon said, looking at the ring and placing a loupe on his eye. *"Ven, Ricardo. Mira."* (Come here, Ricardo. Look.) Simon looked and then handed the ring and the loupe to Ricardo while Juan stayed completely silent. Simon looked again.

"Es EE1." (It's EE1.) Ricardo said.

"No sabes lo que dices" (You don't know what you are saying), Simon said quietly to Ricardo and looked at him with eyes that spoke. He was reprimanding Ricardo for his lack of negotiating instinct, because he had revealed that the diamond had good color, which the lady might not have known. Diamonds that were colorless were rated "D," "E," and "F," with "D" indicating the best quality.

"Es muy bueno y se lo que vale en el mercado.

Pocas tiendas en México tienen la clientela que pueda comprar algo así." (It's very good and I know its value. Few stores in Mexico have the clientele to buy something like this.) Juan said it softly.

"¿Cuánto crees que vale?" (How much do you think it's worth?) Ricardo asked, trying to repair the damage he had caused to his reputation.

"Cincuenta y cinco" (Fifty-five), Juan said.

"¿Qué? ¿Cincuenta y cinco, qué?" (What? Fifty-five what?) Ricardo asked.

"Mil dólares" (Thousand dollars), Juan said.

Ricardo scoffed. His father stayed quiet. They both knew the visitor was spot-on.

"¿Señora?" (Your last name?) Simon asked.

"Rodriguez viuda de Loret. Victoria" (Rodriguez widow of Loret. Victoria), Juan said.

"Pues me gusta la piedra pero no vale lo qué dice." (I like the stone, but it is not worth what you said.) Simon assumed a simple facial expression that no longer allowed Ricardo to speak.

"¿Cuánto me dará?" (How much will you give me?) Juan said.

Simon assessed his options. Buying this quality stone at a distributor would cost him a minimum of forty-five thousand, which had the one advantage that it could be bought with credit. But paying cash offered advantages—if the price was right, he would make more money, and he could get rid of cash he didn't want to deposit in the bank. And if he didn't sell the stone in a timely fashion, it wouldn't accrue interest.

"¿Me permite desmontarla para pesarla?" (Would you allow me to unmount the stone so I can weigh it?) Simon asked.

"OK, mientras yo la vea todo el tiempo." (OK, so

long as it doesn't leave my sight.)

The next few minutes were gut-wrenching for Juan. He was constantly under the eyes of Simon as Ricardo proceeded to unmount the stone. It never left his sight, but he felt Simon's eyes on him. Evidently Simon was trying to place him.

"*¿Note un sonsonete en su voz?*" (Did I detect an accent in your voice?) Simon asked.
"*Viví muchos años en Nuevo Laredo y Laredo.*" (I lived many years in New Laredo and Laredo.) Juan responded with a tone that made them adversaries and tried to discourage any additional chitchat.
"*¿Usted sabe que no le puedo pagar el valor de menudeo de la piedra?*" (You are aware that I cannot pay you the retail value of the stone?)
"*Claro, usted tiene que ganarle.*" (Obviously, you need to profit.)

The scale read 3.58 carats, and all three could see the displayed numbers. Juan remained quiet. He had said 3.5, and it was closer to 3.6 on their scale. This was good for him.

"*Le puedo dar veinticinco*" (I can give you twenty-five), Simon said.
"*Dame treinta y se la dejo. En efectivo*" (Give me thirty and I'll leave it here with you. Cash), Juan said.
"*Efectivo! No, señora, no se puede. Necesito la factura*" (Cash! Impossible. I need a receipt), Simon said.

Juan was happy. He was no longer bargaining price, but payment system. He had thirty locked, and this was a great fence for him.

"*Señor Becker, debe saber que esta es la unica*

posesión que me dejó mi marido que vale algo. Tengo que pagar la universidad de mi hijo y no puedo aceptar menos de treinta. Soy persona física y le doy el recibo que necesite, pero quiero efectivo. No confío en los cheques y no quiero depositar esta cantidad en mi banco. ¿Me entiende?" (Mr. Becker, you should know that this is the only possession my late husband left me of any value. I need to pay my son's college tuition, and I cannot accept anything less than thirty. I can write you the receipt you need, but I need cash. I don't trust checks or banks, and I am not about to deposit that amount in my bank.) Juan said all this in a super-feminine voice full of fears.

"Le doy el efectivo. Treinta. ¿No tiene mas piezas como esta?" (I'll give you cash. Thirty. Do you have more stones like this?) Simon said.

"No. Nunca me vera por aquí otra vez. ¡A menos que me case con Carlos Slim!" (No. You will never see me around here again. Unless I marry Carlos Slim!) Juan said.

Ricardo chuckled at the joke. Simon took a huge mountain of twenty-dollar bills from a safe. The bills were not new, so the packs were bulkier than those of new bills would be. Juan suspected it was drug money from sales to rich dealers and smugglers. Simon looked eager to get rid of it. His secretary prepared a receipt for "Mrs. Victoria Rodriguez, widow of Loret," for Juan to sign. Ricardo placed the cash that wouldn't fit inside Juan's purse into a Becker shopping bag and covered it with gold wrapping paper. Juan sensed that Simon might want to check his identity, but the deal was sealed. Nevertheless, he came up with a request as a way to divert Simon's attention.

"Señor Becker. ¿Me puedo quedar con la montura de mi anillo? Le tengo mucho cariño y pues le puedo poner una zirconia. No sé..." (Mr. Becker. Could I

keep the setting of my ring? It has enormous sentimental value to me and maybe I can mount a zirconia. I don't know...), Juan said, almost crying.

"*Claro, claro que sí*" (Of course, of course you may), Simon said, handing the ring mount back to him.

Juan kissed the stoneless ring and shed a tear. It was a perfect ploy to exploit the emotion of the moment. In Simon and Ricardo's eyes, a widow had sold her only possession of value and lost a sentimental heirloom. How could they ask her for ID? Her tears sufficed. Juan signed the paper with perfect Palmer-style handwriting that he had copied from his mother's style. Every letter of the name was beautifully scrolled and perfectly legible. *V-i-c-t-o-r-i-a L-o-r-e-t.* He handed the receipt to them, grabbed the bag full of cash, and waked sadly out of the office.

"*¿Me pide un taxi? ¿De sitio?*" (Can you call me a cab? A respectable cab?) Juan asked.

"*Claro que sí*" (Of course), Simon said.

Simon asked his secretary to call a cab and saw Juan out of the office. The door closed behind him.

"*Ricardo. ¿Viste?*" (Ricardo. Did you see?) Simon said.

"*¿Qué, Pà? ¿Te gusto?*" (What, Dad? You liked her?) Ricardo asked.

"*No, idiota. El trato que hice. No viste. ¡Esta piedra vale facil sesenta mil bolas!*" (No, idiot. The deal I made. This stone is worth a good sixty thousand clams.)

"*¿No, dijiste que no valía los cincuenta y cinco que ella dijo?*" (I thought you said it wasn't worth the fifty-five she said.)

"*Piensa. ¿3.58 es lo mismo que 3.6 y 3.6 se redondea a que número? ¿Y con una montadura buena, de nuestro estilo? ¿Hmm?"* (Think—3.58 is the same as 3.6, which rounds up to what number? And with a mount made by us, in our style? Hmm?)

"¡Facil los sesenta!" (Sixty thousand easy!) Ricardo got it. It was perfect.

The Beckers doubled their money in a split second. Juan made a year's salary with his first stone. He traveled in the cab to a Starbucks only a few blocks from Becker's. The bathrooms were minimally clean and large. There, he transformed into a man again. It was twice as hard as the last time; ripping the latex from his face was messy. But the wig and dress were easy enough. In his purse under the ten thousand dollars were a T-shirt and a small bag holding razor-thin waterproof pants made by a sporting goods store. He removed the high heels and placed them in a bag that was sewn to the dress he wore. In the very bottom of the handbag was a cheap pair of plastic flip-flops that he put on his feet after removing the pantyhose. Those he sent to the bottom of the trash bin in the bathroom. He left the busy Starbucks as a man carrying a knapsack. Any video would be of her entry and then a man's exit, and with no criminal activity chances were the footage would be deleted in a few days.

He took a cab directly to the Banamex bank where he kept his safe-deposit box. Inside the box viewing room he counted the bills one by one, looking at the hundred-, fifty-, and mostly twenty-dollar bills that Becker had given him. One by one he placed them in the box, and every now and then he omitted a twenty here and there. They added up to exactly 1,180 dollars in counterfeit bills. He sat there thinking what to do. Then he counted out the four thousand five hundred dollars for the security deposit and first month's rent on the condominium he would lease for Virginia.

Finally, he counted out an extra thousand to have as petty cash. He had planned on discarding the counterfeit dollars, but then a new thought occurred to him. Contrary to what he had promised, he would pay Mr. Becker a second visit as Victoria, widow of Loret.

A. A. Dober

TWENTY-FOUR

Brent was furious at Leo. He knew that his case was closed, but having this insurance investigator proving how dumb he was made him mad. Cliff had told him that Leo was interested in the GPS data, but that he had given him the cold shoulder. Brent called in Ivory.

"Did you give any data on the case to Leo?" Brent asked Ivory.

"You mean other than the entire file you asked me to copy and give to him?" Ivory sarcastically asked back.

"Cliff said that Leo wanted the pigeon GPS data. Did you share that with him?"

"No, but..."

"But what?"

"I might have told him Dick Greyson had it," she said, lowering her voice with every syllable.

"Fuck me!"

"That is exactly what Leo was working on last night," Ivory said out loud.

"Come again? What do you mean, last night?"

"Nothing."

"Ivory, you are blushing! Are you seeing former detective Leo Stephens?"

"Kind of."

"Where did you see these papers?"

"Oh, I didn't, but when he got the e-mail, he and I parted ways. He was itching to analyze it."

Brent raised a finger, shushing Ivory. He pushed a line on his phone and spoke.

"Get me Dick Greyson, ASAP."

Almost instantly, Dick entered the office.

"Dick, did you send the GPS data file to Leo?" Brent asked.

"Yes," Dick answered.

"OK. Did you analyze it first?"

"Well, I sent him a copy. I still have the information. It was an e-mail."

"I know how e-mail works. My question is, did you analyze the information first?"

"We saw where the pigeon started and where it ended. It was on the GPS."

"You realize that I know exactly where the pigeon started and exactly where it ended. I was at both places. Physically."

"And?"

"I don't need that file for that information, and neither does Leo Stephens. There is something in that data that he was looking for, and you idiots need to find it as well. So go into your cubicle and analyze the data. I want to find whatever Leo was looking for. Dick and Ivory, get on it together and report to me every hour on the hour."

"I thought you said the case was closed," Dick said.

"I just gave you a direct order. Go!"

They left the office and walked straight to Dick's cubicle to sit and stare at numbers. After a good thirty minutes of not knowing what to do, Dick pleaded.

"Just call him. He can cut this process short. Don't tell him we are looking into it, though," Dick said.

"OK." Ivory was bored and happy to get an excuse to dial Leo's phone.

Brent knew Leo was on to something, and he didn't have the resources to follow every step he would take, but this one came from his office, so he wasn't going to let it go. He called Dick.

"Anything?" Brent asked.

"Nothing." Dick answered as he saw Ivory hanging up and turning her head in a no motion.

Leo was crossing into Mexico and there was no cell service in the border area. Dick and Ivory would have to think this one through on their own.

Meanwhile, Leo was already on his way to the coordinates he'd deciphered earlier that marked the beginning of the change in pattern. Leo arrived at the bridge where Juan had dropped the GPS to the moving truck. He then drove through the neighborhood of poor homes, constantly on the lookout for pigeon aviaries. He couldn't see any. He backtracked from the edge of the ravine to the main street, where Juan's home stood empty. He walked up and down the street until an old black 1980 Dodge Aspen rolled up to him. Two large and rough-looking Mexican men got out and went up to Leo. He did not budge.

"What do you want? Gringo," Buitre's assistant said.

"I am looking for a pigeon aviary around here," Leo said.

The men's faces showed a total lack of emotion. Leo was hoping for a glint or a telling sign that he was on to something.

"What the hell. You think we are stupid?" Buitre's assistant Pinguino asked.
"I didn't say that," Leo replied.
"Get in your car and go back to the States."
"And if I don't?"
"You will regret coming here, asking questions."

Leo had rubbed these thugs the wrong way. They could smell his cop stench. He decided to cut the expedition short. Sometimes survival was the better outcome.

"I was just leaving. No pigeons around here," Leo said.
"Nice of you to come, gringo *pendejo*," Pinguino said.

The insult of the profanity was enough to make Leo go berserk. He was going to leave, but now he would do so after leaving a mark. He turned to go, giving Pinguino and Buitre's other assistant his back. He took one step forward and as the Mexican thugs smiled, assured they had accomplished their goal, Leo turned with precision, speed, and strength, and hit Pinguino directly in the throat; the man went down instantly and posed no more threat than a newborn as he hit the unpaved neighborhood sidewalk. Then Leo ducked the other man's blow and hit him with a left-hand uppercut to the ribs. The rib snapped with a cracking sound, and Leo gave the second man a right-hand punch to the jaw that disabled him.

Leo walked away and got in his car, leaving the area immediately. He knew he had only a few minutes, and he would need them to create enough distance between him and the thugs. These men would not forget him, and if he came back, he would be in real danger. After the beating he'd given them, their next meeting would end with a bullet in his head from a drive-by. Yet the thought of a pigeon aviary somewhere near there was still niggling at him.

If the pigeons had landed there, it would be possible to dismantle the aviary and leave no trace. A criminal would do this. Leo needed, at a minimum, to find neighbors who had seen the birds. The homes were mostly single story with few exceptions. Most looked awful. He left the area of inner roads and went back to the main road to return to the States. An idea struck him as he noticed a crowded bus stop. He parked nearby and walked to the stop. A woman in her thirties sat, waiting, and he sat down next to her.

"*¿Disculpe?*" (Excuse me?) Leo said with a heavy American accent.

"*Digame*" (Tell me), the woman said.

"*¿Usted vive en esa colonia?*" (Do you live in that neighborhood?) Leo asked, pointing at the low-income housing he'd just left.

"*Sí.*"

"*¿No sabe si había una casa de pájaros? ¿No vio pájaros que vivían ahi?*" (Do you know if there was a birdhouse? Did you happen to see birds living there?) Leo asked.

The lady looked confused. She didn't respond. She looked at Leo like he was from outer space.

"Pigeons. Many pigeons." Leo said in English

with a Spanish accent and moved his hands about like
birds.

The lady looked even more confused and pointed to
the birds on the wire.

"*¿Pájaros? ¿Como esos?*" (Birds? Like those?)
the lady asked.
"*Sí. ¡Pigeons!*" Leo said.
"*Pichónes.*"
"*Sí, sí, pichónes. ¿Tu viste?*" (Yes, yes, pigeons.
Did you see any?)
"No."

Dead-ended again. Everyone in the bus stop was
looking curiously. Then a young man came up to Leo.
He was fourteen at most and looked like a typical
young Mexican teenager. Basically a Mexican in
American clothing—jeans, a tie-dyed T-shirt, and a
baseball hat.

"Are you looking for a pigeon home? Like on the
roof of a house?" The kid said in a perfect American
English with absolutely no accent.
"Yes. You speak English?" Leo asked.
"Well, I am American," the kid said.
"You know of a pigeon hutch in your
neighborhood?" Leo said.
"There are a few. You see." The kid pointed to a
flock of small birds circling in the horizon.
"Yeah, I see those. But I am looking for one near
the bridge that crosses the freeway. Back there in that
direction." Leo pointed in the direction of Juan's
home.
"There might be one over there; I don't know."
"I looked in that section and couldn't find one."
"That whole section is owned by Buitre. He
knows everything that happens in that section."

"Buitre?"

"That is his name. If he has a real name I have no idea, but he is the landlord."

"Do you have any idea where I can find this Buitre?"

"He is always around. If not him personally, then his goons. They collect the rent and keep people in line. Like security, but the kind that can hurt you."

"I see. You have been incredibly helpful. Here."

Leo handed the kid a twenty-dollar bill.

"Thank you. Oh, one thing," the kid said.

"Yes?" Leo asked.

"I don't think Buitre speaks English. You are better off finding a Mexican to go with you. Or maybe two."

"Thanks, I'll keep that in mind."

Leo left the bus stop area, went to his car, and drove back across to the States. He knew the two men he had beaten up were Buitre's men, and talking to this guy would not get him anywhere that day. He would send a local insurance adjuster to speak to Buitre and get to the truth on who kept the birds there.

TWENTY-FIVE

Juan was not sure which strategy was better—return to Becker's and complain about the counterfeit cash, or just keep mum and let it go. It was as much money as his Camry had brought in, and now he was considering letting it go. But his resolve proved stronger, and the rush of doing the entire physical transformation also lurked. In the unlikely event that Becker considered reporting the purchase to the insurance companies, to return would really solidify that Mrs. Loret's sale was legitimate.

He dressed again in his motel room and went to Becker's. Inside, the young Mr. Becker was working a couple, and Juan began to look for an item in the range of fifteen hundred dollars to haggle down to the $1,180 he had in false money. He looked for a bracelet that held six or seven stones in two-carat size. He found a bracelet with a band of tiny diamonds surrounding four aquamarine stones. It was perfect, because the aquamarines were semiprecious and he could replace them with real diamonds. He noticed the gems' shape matched some of the ones he had in his inventory. This bracelet would move four two-carat stones. It was priced at 20,000 pesos, which was equivalent to the price he was looking for in dollars. A young saleslady came up to him. Without looking up he talked to her as he pointed at the item.

"¿Puedo ver ese brazalete, por favor?" (May I see that bracelet, please?) Juan asked.
"Claro" (Of course), she replied.

The girl put it on the pad. Juan touched it and gently placed it on his palm. He realized he couldn't try it on because lowering the sleeves on his blouse meant a hairy wrist would show.

"Me lo llevo" (I'll take it), Juan said.
"¡Qué bien!" the saleswoman said, shocked at how easy that sale went.
"Digale al señor Becker que la viuda de Loret lo quiere ver para pagarle en efectivo." (Tell Mr. Becker that the widow of Loret wants to see him, to pay him in cash.)
"El señor Becker no se encuentra." (Mr. Becker is not in.)
"Lo estoy viendo ahi con esos clientes." (But I can see him there talking to those clients.)
"Oh. Usted se refiere a Ricardo." (Oh. You mean Ricardo.)
"Sí."

The saleswoman went to speak to Ricardo. He looked over and acknowledged Mrs. Loret. He took the bracelet from the girl and instructed her to keep tending to his clients, then made his way over to Juan.

"Señora Loret, qué rapido regreso." (Mrs. Loret, you are back so soon.)
"Sí. Pense que debia regresarles el favor

comprándoles algo. Me encanto esa pulsera." (Yes. I thought I should return the favor by buying something. I love this bracelet.)

"Vale veinticinco mil." (It's twenty-five thousand.)

"Pues como ustedes no me pagaron el precio de venta, yo le quiero pedir un descuento. Le doy mil ciento ochenta dólares, que son como veinte mil." (Well, you didn't pay me retail so I would like a discount. I can give you one thousand one hundred and eighty dollars, it's roughly twenty thousand.)

Ricardo paused and thought about the transaction. He was authorized to give discounts and hefty ones; all he had to do was read the code on the bracelet to see what the cost was. He looked at the piece and coyly saw the number code. The actual cost was about half of the list price. If he sold it to Mrs. Loret, he would have profited eight thousand pesos or about five hundred dollars in cash.

"Hecho." (Done.)

"Qué bien, me encanta. ¿Me la pone en una cajita bonita?" (Good, I love it. Can you put it in a nice box?)

"Por supuesto." (Of course.)

Juan took out all the forged bills in a neat bundle and handed them to Ricardo.

"No a mi no. En la caja." (No, don't give it to me. To the cashier.) Ricardo said.

"Ricardo, esta compra es con usted. No necesito recibo" (Ricardo, this purchase is with you. I don't need a receipt), Juan said, taking the little jewelry box Ricardo had prepared and handing him the money. Ricardo took the cash and put it in his folder, and Juan turned 180 degrees and went straight for the door.

Ricardo looked at Mrs. Loret, and his eyes immediately went to the other customers he was neglecting. He quickly went to the cashier and handed him the little white slip that he took from the bracelet and the cash. At that moment he saw that a small yellow light turned on in the showroom ceiling. It was an alert that Mr. Becker was in. He slipped past the customers, telling them they were in good hands with the saleswoman, and went upstairs.

"Pá" (Dad), Ricardo said, entering the office.
"¿Qué paso mi hijo?" (What happened, son?) Mr. Becker said from behind his desk.
"¿Te acuerdas de la señora. Loret? ¿La que dijo que nunca la veríamos por aquí otra vez?" (Do you remember Mrs. Loret, the lady who said she would never come back?)
"¿Sí, y? (Yes, and?)"
"Le acabo de vender un brazalete en veinte mil pesos." (I just sold her a bracelet for twenty thousand pesos.)

The internal phone began to ring at Mr. Becker's desk. He picked up, signaling to Ricardo to quiet down.

"¿Qué? ¿Cuántos? ¿Mil ciento ochenta? ¡No jodas!" (What? How much? One thousand one hundred and eighty! Fuck!) Mr. Becker hung up, furious.
"¿Qué paso?" (What happened?) Ricardo asked, white as a sheet and feeling the blood rush down from his head.
"¡Que te regreso todos los dolares falsos que le dimos, menso! ¡Eso paso!" (That she returned to us all the forged dollars we gave her! That's what happened!)

Ricardo sat speechless in the chair in front of his dad's huge desk.

A. A. Dober

TWENTY-SIX

Leo sent a Mexican insurance agent to find out about Buitre's tenants with the pigeon hutch. He gave him a $500 budget to bribe Buitre. In a few days, his agent called him.

"Leo, I have what you need. But it will cost you," the agent said.

"You need more money? I gave you plenty," Leo said.

"Not really. This Buitre is a real gangster. I ended up giving him a grand. But he spilled the beans."

"A grand! Jesus!"

"You want the intel or not?"

"Yes, I will send you the other five right away. Count on it."

"Virginia Merlo. *M* as in Mary, *E* as in Eduard, *R* as in Robert, *L* as in Luis, and *O* as in Ocean. *Merlo*. Got it?"

"Yes, thanks, my man."

"You are welcome."

Buitre had no trouble giving Virginia's name to some investigator. After all, the Merlos were not doing anything wrong at his property, and dishing out the name would only distance any scrutiny away from his projects.

In a cursory Google name search Leo found out all about Virginia and particularly, her former husband's death and his case with TIPCO. Leo was shocked to find that he was working for TIPCO and reading this. The coincidence was just too strong, and his business frowned on coincidences. She had motive, but it was a male he sought. That is when he did the math on her son. He was only twenty-five years old, and it seemed that someone so young was incapable of an intricate crime like this. But he had the same motive, revenge.

Leo read more. The case stunk and definitely TIPCO looked evil in its treatment of the Merlos. For an moment, he felt he was working for the wrong team. Maybe the Merlos kept the birds for someone else, but in any event, he would need to interview this lady and her son. He requested funds to travel to Mexicali, where the last credit card in the name of Juan Luis Merlo had been used. He began with the motel attendant and ended with the sale of the Camry. The trail was cold after that. Traveling south into Mexico without knowing where they could possibly have gone was ludicrous. There were no pings for any credit cards in her name or her son's from that day onward. It was an impossible search until they surfaced into the system. Leo was not defeated, but now needed to wait until the perpetrator or perpetrators made mistakes. Fencing ten million dollars in retail value of diamonds always surfaced in his system of informants, and he would find them soon enough. For now, though, he was returning empty-handed.

That evening, he called on Ivory and they went to the Outback again. They met in the lobby and kissed. It was the true beginning of a relationship, as he no longer needed anything from her office. She was delighted that he had called and really enjoyed that Brent hated Leo.

"It is so nice to see you again," Leo said.
"Same here. How did it go?" Ivory asked.
"Cold trail."
"But you know who did it?"
"Not really. I have a suspect, but absolutely no proof."
"But that is something. We have no idea who did it. Who is the suspect?"
"You know I can't divulge that information. But I'll let you know once we find him."
"Find him? What do you mean?"
"Well, I think I know who did it, but I have no idea where he is."
"Oh boy. I would love to meet him," she blurted out, immediately regretting having said that.
"You would love to arrest him, you mean. Right?"
"Yes, that is what I meant. Although…"
"What?"
"I am intrigued by the ingenuity of the crime. It was a perfect crime until you found him."
"I said I have a suspect. I can't prove anything."
"He didn't leave much behind. It was masterful!"
"But he does have a fortune in diamonds, and I doubt he'll avoid making mistakes as he cashes them in. That is always how we catch these fools."
"Oh, Leo. I love the way you speak."
"Ivory."

They were a pair of lovebirds. Patrons and staff at the Outback couldn't help but stare at them in envy. True love sprouts in the strangest and most random fashion.

TWENTY-SEVEN
Three years later

Juan Merlo sat at a consigned Louis XVI–style desk, his favorite painting on the wall behind him, Milton Avery's *Paris Pigeons* from 1955. The painting was flanked by two large marble obelisks that sat on a long Biedermeier console with tags everywhere. The desk was full of papers, and an iPad sat in the center. His storefront was now twice as large as when he'd started out, and it contained a maze of small pathways through all sorts of art and antiques. From his desk, he could see the entire store, because he had built a two-step-high office with glass walls. On the store side of the glass, there was a beautiful antique balustrade recovered from a demolished sixteenth-century building in the center of the city. Behind his desk to the right was a door to his private bathroom, and past that bathroom, another secret door that led to the rear parking lot. Juan was still paranoid that someday, someone might investigate him. But the passage of time had made him more relaxed. Having sold all the diamonds also helped. His selling had improved with time, and he had managed to net close to four million dollars. He'd spent it on high-end travel and artifacts for his shop, antiques and art worth about seven million. Art had moved up in value, year after year!

Having a consignment store and a strong paranoia had led him to develop a genius business plan. He actually did consign furniture and art from people, but he kept a separate book for additional consignments. If an inspector came to claim that the inventory he held was worth millions, Juan would produce the false consignment book showing that almost all the valuables belonged to others. When he sold an expensive piece that he had actually bought with diamond money, he would get rid of an item consigned to a client as well. He would show the sale as a small commission for his business, with a large payoff to a private citizen. Rarely did anyone question this sort of transaction, and if an individual was asked whether he did consign a piece to "Antiguedades y Consignaciones Euro-America SA," he truthfully answered yes.

Juan had traveled all over the world and had completed an art history degree at the Instituto de Cultura Superior. He traveled coach to Paris, London, Rome, Rio, Caracas, Lima, Buenos Aires, Montreal, Toronto, Vancouver, Chicago, Dallas, and Seattle and business class to Madrid, Basel, Berlin, Moscow, Prague, Milan, Geneva, Brussels, Amsterdam, Stockholm, New York, Monterrey, Houston, Washington, Boston, and Los Angeles, all to fence a few stones, and always returning with art and antiques that could mask their value. He had used many different looks and disguises, and had left no trace of his real looks in any public or store security video. He traveled with his Mexican passport, as he had dual citizenship, which allowed him to be a tourist in the United States.

His love life improved, and he began dating the daughter of a woman who'd studied at the Art History

Institute with him. His life became tranquil and he treasured that. Meanwhile, his "Lon Chaney" experiences led him to participate in a theater group; the anonymity he'd enjoyed through disguise was an addiction and a craft that he did not want to give up. His girlfriend was beautiful and rich; he was the envy of all his friends. Through her, he felt a true connection to the life his father had promised, a life of entitlement and belonging. One day, she decided to give Juan a new iPad. She bought it with her father's money and set it up in his name. He would love it, she thought.

Over the years, Virginia noticed Juan's great success and wealth and had become a little suspicious. After all, she was in a two-bedroom apartment in Polanco and had a maid. Juan took care of all her bills. But every time she felt she needed to broach the subject, the words eluded her and she actually asked for more money instead. He complied, and she kept her suspicions to herself, eventually buying into the idea that he was a good businessman.

All the anonymity that Juan managed to keep was destroyed the day he received the iPad.

A. A. Dober

TWENTY-EIGHT

An e-mail alert arrived on Leo's desktop computer.

Juan Luis Merlo registered an Apple computer in Mexico City.

Leo's gut seized on the possibilities, and he immediately called for funding to reopen the Quayles case. Quayles had been paid the full appraised cost of the diamonds at seven million dollars; it was a loss on the TIPCO books and a smear to Leo's reputation. TIPCO's CEO, Dennis Avner, did not allow the reopening of the case, and Leo had no budget with which to follow the latest lead. Leo was not happy, but he was resourceful. He called his fiancée immediately.

"Baby, how about a trip to Mexico City?" Leo asked.

"What? Why Mexico City?" Ivory said.

"I hear it is a beautiful city. Don't you want to go?"

"I'll go with you to wherever you take me."

"That's the spirit."

Leo told Ivory his real intentions on the three-hour

flight from Lindbergh Field. This was a fact-finding mission and a vacation combined. Ivory felt a strange butterfly sensation in her gut when she learned they would finally meet the mastermind of the Fly Diamonds case. She was all in.

The Maria Isabel Sheraton Hotel was a hub for the American traveler to Mexico City. It was a block away from the American Embassy on Paseo de la Reforma, the main artery connecting the downtown to the suburbs. It was an old hotel, but continually upgraded to offer all the amenities the modern traveler required. The food was safe and delicious and the service impeccable, all at an affordable cost. A hotel stay this luxurious in the United States would have cost at least three times as much.

Leo had the address of the business registered for the computer, and the day after their arrival, they took an Uber to Antiguedades y Consignaciones Euro-America SA at exactly eleven in the morning when the store opened. They arrived in the Polanco neighborhood to find the store open, but with only one employee in charge. A very pretty young female who seemed to know exactly how to manage the business of selling greeted them. Leo found out from her that the owner usually came around five in the afternoon, to check on sales and deliveries, and that he was indeed Juan Luis Merlo.

Leo and Ivory decided to sightsee and went to the Museum of Archaeology and later to lunch at a famous restaurant. They felt the city's high elevation when they drank their first tequila cocktail. The thin air contained less oxygen, so the alcohol kicked hard. Soon, they were forgetting all about the mission and enjoying themselves. It was supposedly a dangerous city, but in every respect the tourist areas seemed perfectly safe. Leo was an experienced traveler and could navigate any situation with ease. At around six in the evening, Ivory noticed that they were running late to see Juan Luis. She showed Leo her wristwatch.

"Shit. Let's get going," Leo said.

Leo spoke to Ivory during the Uber ride to the shop.

"I want you to look around and act as if you are going to buy something. We should look like a regular couple, and I will try and feel out if my hunch is right," Leo instructed.
"I can do that," Ivory said, and hiccupped.
"I wonder if we should do this tomorrow."
"What if he doesn't come to work tomorrow?"
"Let's do this," Leo reiterated.

Inside the shop, Juan was sitting at his desk when he saw the tipsy Americans enter the shop. They looked around and he noticed his gaze on them. The man immediately darted toward Juan, leaving his girlfriend to browse. Juan moved swiftly to meet him before he arrived at his office, but Leo was fast and arrived at the office faster.

"How can I help you?" Juan asked as Leo stood at the threshold of the office door.
"We are just browsing, but I was wondering if you had jewelry. You see that pretty girl down there?" Leo asked.
"Yes."
"Well, I am looking to get engaged. Nothing says 'I love you' like a diamond."
"I am afraid you have the wrong shop, then. We are not jewelers."
"I am sorry, you are Juan Luis Merlo, right?"
"I am."

"I was told you sold diamonds?"

"I'm afraid whoever told you that misinformed you. I have never sold a diamond in my life. I don't invest in jewelry of any kind. Look around. I deal in antiques and art."

"I can see that. This is an incredible store you have."

"Thank you. Now if you don't mind, Soledad, my assistant talking to your fiancée over there, can help you." Juan made a motion indicating Leo should exit his office.

"I see you have a painting of pigeons," Leo exclaimed, pointing at the Milton Avery.

"Yes, so?"

"How much is it?"

"Too much. It is not for sale."

"Too much? What do you mean?"

"That, my friend, is a Milton Avery from 1955. *Paris Pigeons.*"

"How much is it worth?"

"Like I said. It is not for sale."

"But if it were, what is its value?"

"I said, friend, it is not for sale, and Soledad can answer any questions you have. I need to get back to work. Please." Juan pointed to Leo for an expected exit.

"I know it's you," Leo said softly, almost inaudibly.

"Please, my friend, I need to get back to my work," Leo said.

"I know it was you."

"Come again? What are you talking about?"

"The diamond heist in San Diego. Three years ago," Leo said, looking at Juan directly in the eye.

"I don't think so."

"You were in the area at the time. I know you lived in a home that housed pigeons until that day."

"They were not my pigeons."

"You took care of them."

"I had to."

"You mean like, at gunpoint?"

"Something like that. I just kept them alive," Juan answered, moving behind his desk and assessing whether this gringo had backup outside.

"Why did you move here so suddenly?"

"Suddenly? I had to save for over two years to move my mom back here."

"Virginia? How is she? Does she know who you are? How can you afford all this?"

"I started this shop selling my mom's Dalí prints. I have found something I am good at. Like the Milton Avery, if you only knew how little I paid for it, you would die. Mexico is a gold mine in antiques and art. People sell well below market price."

"How much is it worth?" Leo asked again.

"You are in insurance, right?" Juan asked.

"Yes, I am."

"Then you should know Avery."

"I don't."

"Let me tell you, an Avery of similar size just sold at auction for fifty thousand. I can sell this one with a nice profit at forty-five. But it is not for sale."

"Forty-five thousand pesos? What is that, like three grand?" Leo asked.

"Dollars."

"Come again? You mean forty-five thousand dollars for that painting? Wow! I can't afford that."

"And you are looking for diamonds?"

"Yes, well I am looking for something small, under ten Gs…but aren't you afraid someone might steal it?" Leo asked, pointing at the Avery.

"Not particularly. Art is hard to sell and it's insured anyway."

"Who is your carrier?"

"Lloyds. They probably sell a piece of my policy to your company. You know how they are. All spreading out the risk so that any hit is meaningless to any given company."

"You seem to know a lot about insurance. Do you know, they are relentless until they recover their losses."

"Are you saying they never take any losses?"

"Oh, natural disasters, yes. Those are losses. But jewelry and art, now that is something they will keep looking for. You have any diamonds?"

"My friend, as I said, you are far from any diamonds here. I specialize in art and antiques."

"Tell me more about your pigeons."

"Well, Avery is the Matisse of American art. He never veered off to follow pure abstraction like his friend Rothko or de Kooning; he kept making what he loved and got better and better at it. Like a good wine."

"I was talking about your real pigeons in Tijuana, Juan," Leo's tone changed.

"They belonged to Buitre. You can go to Tijuana and talk to him," Juan said, sitting down at his desk and looking at papers.

Juan was trying to act as cool as possible and knew that he could always escape through the back. He looked at Ivory through the glass talking to Soledad about a santo figure.

"Buitre gave you up," Leo said.

"That is nonsense. Buitre can't say anything bad about me. He is a criminal and taking his word over mine is ludicrous," Juan said calmly and added, "Your fiancée seems to be interested in a seventeenth-century sculpture. If I were you, I would pop that question soon."

"What do you mean?"

"You are blind, my friend. For an insurance investigator, you are clearly not very observant."

"What are you talking about?"

"What is your name?"

"Leo."

"And hers?"

"Ivory."

"Listen, Leo, Ivory there is carrying a little Leo or Leona. You better marry her before she carries the baby to term. You want that baby to have a father, don't you?"

"What? How can you know that?"

"Observing is what I do. I can tell if a picture frame is new or one hundred years old. Look at her. She walked in and made a face when she smelled those flowers in the vase. It was almost like she was going to puke. Then she met Soledad there and she showed interest only in sculpture and particularly in the putti there. You see?"

"You are sure she is pregnant?" Leo flushed with happiness.

"She didn't tell you?"

"But she drank tequila."

"Then she doesn't know either. She is not very connected to her body. Is she in a harsh profession?"

"She is a police officer."

"It figures."

"Wow…" Leo was speechless and sat down on a chair across from Juan.

"Would you like to buy that putti for her? I can have it shipped to your home without her knowledge so when she gets home it can surprise her. Like your baby will surprise you," Juan said.

"But shouldn't I tell her I know?"

"You are going to tell her that your suspect figured it out? She would think you are crazy. I'll tell you what. Go to a pharmacy and buy a test, which is the way to be sure. Tell her you had a hunch. Then you can celebrate. You will never forget Mexico City."

"You sure those pigeons belonged to Buitre?"

"I kept them alive for Buitre, but who knows if

they were his?"

"Did you know the pigeons were part of a heist? A diamond heist?"

"No? Really?" Juan was mocking Leo.

"The Fly Diamonds heist."

"I remember the day of the heist exactly. I was working at the Savory Yolk, and we saw the helicopter hovering over Quayles Jewels. You can ask Finch. He is the manager of the Savory Yolk, I was there with him when the TV reported the whole story."

"So you have an alibi."

"Rock solid. Tori the news reporter was explaining how the criminals were still inside the store when Finch and I were watching. Ask him."

Leo realized Juan was smart and perceptive and felt a sense of respect. He felt lucky to meet someone like Juan, a somewhat polar opposite of himself but of similar intellect.

"May I introduce you to her?" Leo asked.

"Sure," Juan said.

They walked the length of the store to meet Ivory by the putti wooden sculpture that had captivated her.

"It is a seventeenth-century piece. Italian. Probably brought to Mexico by a viceroy to decorate the castle in Chapultepec Park. Have you visited the castle yet?" Juan asked Ivory.

"No."

"Oh, you must have Leo take you; no visit to Mexico City can skip that. I am Juan. Enchanted to meet you." Juan took her hand and kissed it.

"Ivory," Ivory introduced herself.

"I know," Juan said.

"Why must we go to the castle?" Leo asked.

"Well, my friend, the castle is built on a

mountaintop where an ancient pyramid used to stand. They actually used the stones hauled by the Aztecs up there to build the foundation." Juan looked directly at Ivory when he said this. "It is in the middle of the equivalent of your Central Park in New York, and all major battles have involved the capture of this castle. Up until the 1930s, it was the home of the president, so in essence it was our White House. Now a museum, luckily."

"Wow. We should go, honey." Ivory was impressed by Juan.

"I know you think I am the Fly Diamonds thief, but your hubby here is quite wrong. He is barking up the wrong tree. Do you want to know the price of the putti?"

Ivory was taken aback. She didn't expect Leo would reveal their intentions and didn't know what to do. The pause was uncomfortably long.

"How much is the putti?" Leo asked.

"Twenty-five thousand pesos, about two grand," Juan said.

"Whoa wee. That is a pretty penny," Leo said.

"But I can give you a great discount, special for Leonardo only," Juan said.

"Give me a second," Leo said.

Ivory was looking at Leo, flushed and visibly uncomfortable. Leo tugged at her arm, and they moved away from Juan's earshot.

"It's not him," Leo said.

"Are you sure?" Ivory asked.

"No. But I think I am dropping this investigation."

"But why?"

"I just don't think I can get this guy. If it is him, we have nothing to go on. He is too smart, and it just feels wrong. Like we are barking up the wrong tree!"

Ivory raised her eyebrows and shoulders in a gesture that implied she didn't care anyway.

"What kind of discount for Leonardo?" Leo asked Juan.
"I will give you a super discount. Give me one thousand and I will wrap it right now."
"Can it go through customs?"
"Of course; art is tax-free going to the States, and this piece is Italian, so you are not transporting a national treasure out of Mexico. You can just carry it or put it in your luggage."

Leo paid three hundred dollars more for the putti than Juan had paid when he bought it from an estate sale about thirty days earlier. Juan had Soledad wrap the baby sculpture in protective plastic wrap, and he handed Ivory a catalog of the most important seventeenth-century buildings in Mexico City.

"Don't forget, Ivory, that Mexico was the richest country in the world in the seventeenth century. We had so much gold that we began the concept of inflation for the Spanish Crown. Please enjoy Mexico, and have a safe trip back to San Diego," Juan said to Ivory as they walked out to the sidewalk.
"Remember, Leo. Test and no alcohol. Got it?" Juan said.
"Yes. Got it. Many, many thanks," Leo said.
"Thank you," Juan said, counting the hundred-dollar bills.

As soon as the lovebirds left, Juan called Virginia.

"Ma. ¿No vas a creer lo que paso" (You are not going to believe what happened), Juan said.

"¿Qué mi hijo?" (What, my son?) Virginia inquired.

"Que somos ricos. Muy ricos. Y nadie no los va a quitar jamás." (That we are rich. Very rich. And nobody will take it from us, ever.)

"¡No te vayas a salar, mi hijo!" (Don't brag; you might get unlucky!)

"¡Ay, ma, siempre negativa tu!" (Oh, Mom, always so negative!)

In the Uber, Ivory wondered.

"What did he mean by test and no alcohol?" Ivory asked.

"Oh, I'll tell you in a moment. Driver? Do you speak English?" Leo asked.

"Yes."

"Can you stop by a pharmacy on the way to the hotel?"

"Sure."

THE END

A. A. Dober

ABOUT THE AUTHOR

A.A. Dober wrote *Fly Diamonds* in 2015. He is the author of *Ultimatus: A Gaming Corporation* his debut novel, and *AmEarth.* He lives in Southern California with his wife and two children.

www.ingramcontent.com/pod-product-compliance
Lightning Source LLC
Chambersburg PA
CBHW031423250626
47155CB00004B/1600